Praise for
Violets Are Blue

"*Violets Are Blue* will break your heart and then piece it back together with infinite care. Barbara Dee expertly captures the struggle to be known and loved within a narrative that presents the complicated reality of addiction. Both Wren and her mother will stay with you long after this story is done."
—Jamie Sumner, author of *Roll with It* and *Tune It Out*

"Barbara Dee tunes into issues that impact middle schoolers and writes about them with compassion, insight, and just plain excellent storytelling. I loved this absorbing, accessible novel, which explores the heartbreaking effects of opioid addiction while also celebrating the joys of discovering a passion and finding people who understand you."
—Laurie Morrison, author of *Up for Air* and *Saint Ivy*

"Barbara Dee has done it again! *Violets Are Blue* is an emotionally rich story that masterfully weaves life's messy feelings while gently and thoughtfully tackling the difficult subject of opioid addiction. Beautiful. Complicated. And full of heart. A must read!"
—Elly Swartz, author of *Smart Cookie* and *Give and Take*

"Told realistically and with compassion, *Violets Are Blue* provides a fascinating look into the world of special effects makeup, budding friendships, family, and the secrets we keep."
—Melanie Sumrow, author of *The Inside Battle* and *The Prophet Calls*

"*Violets Are Blue* tackles the subject of addiction with hope and compassion. Readers will cheer for Wren in this story about family bonds broken and redefined, learning to trust, and being true to yourself. I loved it!"
—Lynne Kelly, author of *Song for a Whale*

Praise for
My Life in the Fish Tank

"I loved *My Life in the Fish Tank*. Once again, Barbara Dee writes about important topics with intelligence, nuance, and grace. She earned all the accolades for *Maybe He Just Likes You* and will earn them for *My Life in the Fish Tank* too."
—Kimberly Brubaker Bradley, author of Newbery Honor Books
Fighting Words* and *The War That Saved My Life

"I felt every beat of Zinny Manning's heart in this authentic and affecting story. Barbara Dee consistently has her finger on the pulse of her middle-grade audience. Outstanding!"
—Leslie Connor, author of *A Home for Goddesses and Dogs* and
National Book Award finalist *The Truth as Told by Mason Buttle*

"*My Life in the Fish Tank* is a powerful portrayal of a twelve-year-old dealing with her sibling's newly discovered mental illness. Author Barbara Dee deftly weaves in themes of friendship, family, and secrets, while also reminding us all to accept what we can't control. I truly loved every moment of this emotional and gripping novel, with its notes of hope that linger long after the last page."
—Lindsay Currie, author of
The Peculiar Incident on Shady Street* and *Scritch Scratch

"*My Life in the Fish Tank* rings true for its humor, insight, and honesty. Zinny is an appealing narrator, and her friendships with supporting characters are beautifully drawn."
—Laura Shovan, author of *Takedown* and
A Place at the Table

"Barbara Dee offers a deeply compassionate look at life for twelve-year-old Zinny, whose older brother faces mental health challenges. This touching novel will go a long way in providing understanding and empathy for young readers. Highly recommended."
—**Donna Gephart, award-winning author of *Lily and Dunkin* and *The Paris Project***

Also by BARBARA DEE

Haven Jacobs Saves the Planet

My Life in the Fish Tank

Maybe He Just Likes You

Everything I Know About You

Halfway Normal

Star-Crossed

Truth or Dare

The (Almost) Perfect Guide to Imperfect Boys

Trauma Queen

This Is Me From Now On

Solving Zoe

Just Another Day in My Insanely Real Life

VIOLETS ARE BLUE

BARBARA DEE

ALADDIN

NEW YORK LONDON TORONTO SYDNEY NEW DELHI

ALADDIN

An imprint of Simon & Schuster Children's Publishing Division
1230 Avenue of the Americas, New York, New York 10020
First Aladdin paperback edition August 2022
Text copyright © 2021 by Barbara Dee
Cover illustration copyright © 2021 by Erika Pajarillo
Also available in an Aladdin hardcover edition.
All rights reserved, including the right of reproduction in whole or in part in any form.
ALADDIN and related logo are registered trademarks of Simon & Schuster, Inc.
For information about special discounts for bulk purchases, please contact
Simon & Schuster Special Sales at 1-866-506-1949 or business@simonandschuster.com.
The Simon & Schuster Speakers Bureau can bring authors to your live event. For
more information or to book an event contact the Simon & Schuster Speakers Bureau
at 1-866-248-3049 or visit our website at www.simonspeakers.com.
Designed by Heather Palisi
The text of this book was set in Odile.
Manufactured in the United States of America 0722 OFF
2 4 6 8 10 9 7 5 3 1
The Library of Congress has cataloged the hardcover edition as follows:
Names: Dee, Barbara, author.
Title: Violets are blue / by Barbara Dee.
Description: First Aladdin hardcover edition. | New York : Aladdin, 2021. |
Audience: Ages 9-13. | Summary: Twelve-year-old Wren, who is learning special effects
makeup, is thrilled to be makeup artist for her new school's production of Wicked, but her
parents' divorce is seriously affecting her mother.
Identifiers: LCCN 2020049088 | ISBN 9781534469181 (hardcover) |
ISBN 9781534469204 (ebook)
Subjects: CYAC: Makeup artists—Fiction. | Theatrical makeup—Fiction. | Theater—Fiction. |
Mothers and daughters—Fiction. | Remarriage—Fiction. | Moving, Household—Fiction.
Classification: LCC PZ7.D35867 Vio 2021 | DDC [Fic]—dc23
LC record available at https://lccn.loc.gov/2020049088
ISBN 9781534469198 (pbk)

This one is for Ripley,
and for all our furry family members,
past and present, near and far

Click

Hey, guys, Cat FX here. Sorry if my voice sounds funny—my allergies are going full blast this morning.

Also, I couldn't sleep. So I spent the night thinking what I wanted to say to you, and here it is: It's really important not to overdo stuff, okay? Yes, I know it's exciting when you have all these shiny new products to play with, and you want to use everything all at once. But trust me on this, it's better to go slowly, adding layer on top of layer, building your character from the inside out. Know what I mean?

Also—and guys, I can't stress this enough— try not to be too obvious. Have fun with these techniques. Experiment, take risks, but always leave room for a bit of mystery.

∘ ○ ∘

Tonight my face was Seafoam Blue.

Not my whole face. Just a light swish across my forehead, the tops of my cheekbones, and around my chin.

The trick was to go slowly, like Cat FX said, applying layer on top of layer. Better to add than to subtract. Build the character from the inside out.

And to be who I imagined—my mental mermaid—I couldn't just slather on a ton of blue pigment. My mermaid's superpower was a kind of camouflage: blending into her surroundings. Slipping undetected through sunken ships. Escaping deadly sea monsters. Coming up for air when necessary.

The other thing I'd decided was that she was a collector. So when she won a battle, or discovered buried treasure, she would always decorate herself with souvenirs. To never forget what she'd been through, what she'd seen. To make it part of herself forever.

Which was why I was gluing a plastic pearl to my eyebrow when I heard the *GRRRRUUUNNNCCCHHH*.

My stomach clenched.

We'd been living here for almost three months, and I still couldn't get used to the awful grinding sound of the garage door.

But at least it gave me warning. Before Mom could get all the way upstairs, I tossed the jar of Seafoam Blue face pigment, the eye shadow in Cyber Purple, the waterproof eyebrow pencil in Medium Brown, and the spidery false eyelashes into my secret makeup kit. Then I slid it under my bed, all the way to the farthest corner, tossing in an old sneaker to hide it.

The shoebox marked *M* stayed on my desk. Visible.

I checked the clock. Only 8:35.

Mom clomped up the stairs in her thick-soled Jungle Mocs, which I'm pretty sure is the official footwear of ER nurses when they aren't wearing sneakers. Just in time, I beat her to the door of my bedroom.

"Hey, honeybee," she called as she reached the top step. In her wrinkled spearmint-green scrubs, she looked droopy, like a plant you forgot to water.

When she smiled, you could see how hard her face was working. "Is that the mermaid?" she asked, lightly touching my cheek.

"Yeah," I said. Mom could always tell the effect I was going for, even when I was in the middle of a character. "Although I'm not totally sure about the color."

"You're not? What's wrong with it?"

"I don't know. The Seafoam Blue seems wrong. Too greenish, maybe? And I'm not getting that shimmery underwater effect. I followed all the directions, but . . ." I shrugged. "It's not how I thought."

"Well, I think it looks really great so far. And I love that eyebrow pearl." She pushed her too-long bangs out of her eyes. "You finished your homework, Wren?"

"Yep. An hour ago."

She looked past me, into my room. Could she see the makeup kit under my bed? No, that was impossible. But of course she could see the shoebox marked M—on my desk, like usual.

"And did your friend Poppy come over after school?" Mom always called her "your friend Poppy," like she thought she needed to remind me that everything was different now: I had a real friend.

"Mom, Poppy has soccer. Remember I told you?" *At least twice. No, more than that.* "And why are you home so early?" *Again.*

"Another mix-up with scheduling. My supervisor keeps overstaffing." Mom leaned against my door and shut her eyes.

For a few seconds I just watched her. With all the changes in her schedule, I knew she hadn't been sleeping well. Not during the night, anyway.

So it didn't shock me to see her so tired. Still, it was a little awkward, both of us just standing there, not talking. Not moving.

"Mom," I said.

Her eyes fluttered open. When she took a step, her knee buckled, or something. She grabbed the doorknob to keep from falling.

"You okay?" I said quickly.

"I'm fine." A small wince. "Just my stupid knee acting up again. Don't worry about it, Wren. I have an early shift tomorrow, so I think I'll just take some Advil and get into bed. Will you please walk Lulu so she can pee?"

Lulu was our three-legged French bulldog. She peed sixteen times a day, and that's no exaggeration.

"Sure," I told her. "Go rest, Mom. And put a pillow under your knee."

"Hey, I'll be the nurse around here, not you." She threw me a little smile as she disappeared into her bedroom.

I waited, and then I heard it: *Click.*

One day while I was at school, Mom had a lock put on her door. To keep the cat off her bed, she'd explained. Although, really, that made no sense, because our one-eyed cat, Cyrus, was too old to jump that high anyway.

And now, every time I heard that sound—*click*—my heart flipped over, but I couldn't say why.

I returned to the mirror propped up on my desk, in front of the shoebox. The mermaid looked blurry now, out of focus, the Seafoam fading into boring pink skin.

5

And the funny thing about makeup effects? They were all just technique, Cat FX said, not magic. But sometimes if you stopped in the middle, it was like you were breaking a spell—and no matter how hard you tried, you couldn't get it back.

I wiped my face and went downstairs to get Lulu's leash.

Changes

There are two kinds of makeup effects: the kind that conceal and the kind that reveal.

As a makeup artist, I'm not about concealing. And I truly believe there's no such thing as a facial flaw or imperfection.

What I'm about—what I'm all about—is revealing something true. Something deep inside, that maybe you didn't even know existed. But that you need to share with the world.

The day Dad left us, just a little over nine months ago, it all happened fast. One gray Saturday morning in February, when we were still living in the house in Abingdon, I woke up to the sound of loud arguing in the kitchen. Yelling,

actually, which happened a lot those days, followed by a car zooming out of our driveway.

At breakfast Mom was drinking coffee in her favorite red mug and reading her phone. Just like she did every regular morning.

"Where's Dad?" I asked.

"Taking a Lyft to the airport," Mom said, still reading. "I'm sure he'll call you as soon as he can."

Were her hands shaking? Her face looked pale. Although she was looking down at her phone, so it was hard to be sure.

"What's going on?" My voice sounded like a five-year-old's, like a squeaky little mouse.

Mom looked up to give me a small, pinched smile. "We'll talk about it, Rennie. But later, because . . ." Her voice trailed off.

"You had a fight? With Dad?"

She didn't answer that specific question. Instead she stood and kissed my forehead. "I don't want you to worry, sweetheart, okay? Everything will be fine, I promise."

Then she put her mug in the sink and left the kitchen.

I waited at the table, but she didn't come back. In fact, I could hear her upstairs in her bedroom, opening and shutting dresser drawers, like she was searching for something, or maybe throwing things away. Pretty soon I figured out that she wanted to be alone, and that I shouldn't knock on her door to ask more questions.

I told myself that if something really serious or important had happened, Mom would just come right out and tell me—wouldn't she? And wouldn't Dad, too? Besides, Dad traveled a lot for his job selling software to companies, so it wasn't completely strange that he'd taken a plane on a weekend morning. Although it *was* strange that he hadn't said goodbye; he'd never left without an early morning hug at the very least.

A few hours later my phone rang. And that was when my stomach knotted, because if my sort-of-friend Annika wanted to talk, she always texted. Mom did too, when she was at the hospital. So for a second I didn't even recognize my ringtone. That it belonged to me, I mean.

But it was Dad; he'd just landed at JFK, and was in a taxi on the way to Brooklyn.

"So Mom told you?" he asked.

"Not really," I said. "I think she's too upset. Dad, what's going on?"

He paused. "It's not something we should discuss over the phone."

Now my heart was banging. "Okay. So when exactly *will* we—"

"Rennie, Mom will talk to you and so will I, but in

person. And I'll see you very, very soon. We both can't wait for you to visit, jellybean. We'll show you around the city and have lots of fun."

He was using so many strange words that bounced off my brain like hailstones: "Visit." "Soon." "City." "Fun." But I picked just one.

"Who's 'we'?" I asked.

"Me and Vanessa." The bad cell service made his voice sound whooshy, like he was going through a fun-house tunnel. Maybe he was. "The woman I met at that software convention in October. I think I mentioned we did a panel together . . . ?"

"No."

"Well, I'm sure I did, jellybean." Now I heard a sound like bubble wrap popping. And then: "We'll talk more later, in person. I love you very much. Always have and always will."

I was too shocked to answer. Had Dad ever told me about any Vanessa? I was pretty sure if he'd said something like, *Hey, jellybean, I've been hanging out with a woman WHO IS NOT MOM,* I'd have processed that information. Although maybe he'd said it in a way I didn't get. Or maybe I wasn't really listening.

"All right, gotta go now," Dad said. "I love you, Rennie."

"I love you too," I said. There was more crackling on the line, so I couldn't tell if he'd even heard it. But then my phone beeped, which meant the conversation was dropped anyway.

Mom was normalish for around a week. I say *ish* because how normal is it to not talk about a missing husband? But she didn't need to specifically tell me that she and Dad had broken up, because by now it was pretty obvious. One time I even said "when you get divorced"—just tossed the word "divorced" into the middle of a sentence, like a firecracker—and she didn't correct me, or even blink.

So I thought: *Okay, that's it, then. Divorce.*

After that first week she started marathon sleeping.

Being an ER nurse meant Mom had weird schedules that were constantly changing, so at first I didn't notice all the napping. But one day I left for school with her still in bed, and when I got home, she was fast asleep on the sofa, cuddled up with Cyrus, wearing pajamas from the night before. On our old kitchen phone were two messages from her supervisor: *Kelly, how's that flu? We need to know when you're coming back to work.* And: *Kelly, I tried your cell twice, but you aren't answering. I also left you three texts. Please return this call immediately—*

I poked Mom's shoulder. "What's going on?" I asked. My voice was loud enough to startle Cyrus, who jumped off the sofa to sit on my foot. "You have the flu?"

"No, just resting." Mom's voice sounded funny. Foggy or something.

"But you told your boss you had the flu? How come?"

Mom ignored that question. "Did your father call you?"

Sometime lately—I couldn't remember when—she'd stopped saying "Dad" and had started saying "your father."

I shook my head.

"Well, sweetheart, he wants you to visit. In Brooklyn. For spring break."

Spring break? That was only two weeks away!

My heart skittered. "He does? But how would I get there? Are you coming too?"

"No, of course not," she said softly. "Anyhow, you're almost twelve; you'll be just fine flying on your own. The flight attendants will watch out for you on the plane, and he'll be right there when you land."

"Okay." I swallowed. "But I won't go if you don't want me to."

Finally, Mom sat up. "Where'd you get that idea?"

"I don't know. Don't be mad, I'm just saying—"

"I'm not mad, Rennie. Anyway, you *have* to visit. He's your father."

She'd said it again: not "Dad," but "your father." A change that was small but felt very big.

In Person

Makeup should never be so heavy that your face can't move. If you're piling on too many effects, your face won't be able to show emotion, and then what you have is just a mask.

And that's basically the opposite of what this is about!

So I flew to New York out of Chicago O'Hare Airport, my first plane trip all by myself. I was scared, but also incredibly excited. And I was so relieved that the flight attendants didn't fuss all over me, like I was wearing a sign that said UNACCOMPANIED CHILD OF SEPARATED PARENTS. Other than smiling at me a little extra, offering me bags of pretzels and chocolate chip cookies, and reminding me where the bathroom was (like I couldn't figure that out on my own), they pretty much ignored me. I guessed they were used to kids making this sort of trip—for example, my sort-of-friend Annika, whose dad lived somewhere sunny in California.

When I landed, Dad was waiting at the exit, just like Mom said he would be. He smothered me in a hug. "Oh, jellybean, I've really missed you," he said.

"I missed you too," I admitted. I'd planned a whole speech about how mad I felt about the way he'd left, how sad I was that our family was broken. But smelling his Dad smell, being in that warm hug, made me blank out on the words.

He drove us (new car! leather seats! giant cup holders!) to where he was living now with Vanessa. His new home—a brownstone in Brooklyn—was skinny and fancy and tall, with a complicated chandelier in the front hallway. The building reminded me of a snobby society lady, like the ones you see in old black-and-white movies.

And it hit me: This Vanessa was rich. Not like us.

Although "us" didn't include Dad anymore. Just Mom and me. And Cyrus and Lulu.

I could feel my palms start to sweat. "So is she here?"

Dad smiled. "You mean Vanessa? Yes, but right now she's resting."

Resting? I thought. *But that sounds exactly like Mom.*

Dad showed me what he said would be my room—a small rectangle on the second floor, with walls painted butter yellow, a white bureau over by the window, and a futon covered by a pale blue quilt with a kite pattern. On the wall were two small paintings. One looked like a sky crammed full of bunny-shaped clouds. The other looked like a lawn filled with blurry dandelions—if that was even what they were. Whoever had painted this wasn't big on details.

Ugh, I thought. A room for a six-year-old, not a sixth grader.

I think Dad saw me notice the paintings. "Of course, you can decorate it any way you like," he said quickly. "In fact, Vanessa thought we'd take you shopping while you're here. So you can make your own choices."

My own choices? But how is any of this my choice?

"Renata? Is that you?" A small woman with long, dark hair appeared in the doorway. In the light I couldn't see her well, but she was wearing a big, flowy sort of dress. This was Vanessa. Obviously.

I glanced at Dad, who was grinning so hard it was embarrassing.

"No one calls me Renata," I heard myself saying. "I *hate* that name, actually."

Right away Dad's grin disappeared. "You do? Since when?"

"Since always! It sounds like a snobby old lady." Probably not the best time to be bringing this up, but I was too nervous to think straight.

Vanessa was still smiling—but she also seemed nervous, I thought. Which was surprising, because I was just a kid. Why would she be nervous about *me*?

"Is it okay if I call you Ren?" she asked. "And if I give you a hug?"

I couldn't look at Dad, so I walked into Vanessa's hug. She was about my height, and as my arms reached behind her, I touched the thick, silky hair that went all the way down her back. Also, I could feel her belly—round and hard.

The belly startled me. *Is she pregnant? She has to be.*

I pulled away. And now I could see that Vanessa was beautiful in an almost mermaid sort of way. Smooth, glowing medium-brown skin with no worry lines, full lips with maybe a trace of gloss. Younger than Mom. A bit tired-looking, with dark shadows under her almond-shaped eyes. But happy. Beaming, actually. Just like Dad was again.

Why are they both so smiley?

"Rennie, we have something to tell you," Dad said gently.

Vanessa raised her eyebrows at him, like: *You sure you want to tell her now?*

"All right," I said. *She's going to say she's pregnant, like it isn't completely obvious.* "Go ahead."

Vanessa took my clammy hands and held them in her warm ones. "It's very happy news; at least, we're happy, and we hope you will be too." She looked at Dad like, *Okay, your turn.*

"Ren," Dad said. "Vanessa and I are getting married at the end of August, and we want you to be maid of honor."

"Me?" My mouth had dried up. "But I thought the maid of honor is the bride's best friend. Or someone like that."

"It's just supposed to be an important person. And who's more important to us than you?"

"But—you—" I was so shocked I couldn't even form a sentence. "You and Mom aren't even divorced yet."

Dad's mouth twitched. "Sweetheart, the divorce is already pretty far along. Mom and I have actually been discussing it for a while now. We think—Mom and I *both* think—it's best for everyone not to drag this out."

All I could do was nod. I mean, I knew a divorce would be happening. But maybe sometime in the far-off future.

"I'm so sorry, Rennie," Dad said quietly. "I know it's hard to believe this, but we're all still a family. And I'll always be there for you, and for Mom, too. Even after."

You mean "after the divorce," so why not say it? I thought. Although, to be fair to Dad, Mom had a hard time with that word too.

When I just shrugged, Dad glanced at Vanessa. "Well.

There's some other big news we were waiting to share with you, but we wanted to do it in person. Vanessa is pregnant. With twins. Isn't that something?"

Am I supposed to be surprised? Does he think I don't notice her belly?

"Yeah, it's something," I said stupidly. "Does Mom know?"

Dad blinked. "Not yet."

"Well, you have to tell her, Dad. You shouldn't keep it a secret. And she'll find out anyway."

All of a sudden, he looked like he was about five years old. By that I mean it was like his eyes were too big for his face, like the proportions were all wrong for a grown-up.

"Yes, I know that, jellybean," he said.

Catwoman

After I got home from Brooklyn, Mom never said anything like, *Oh, by the way, I heard the news—all of it, including about the babies.* But the way she was not-talking about Dad, I knew she knew. And if I ever mentioned him, she immediately changed the subject. She wasn't marathon sleeping anymore, but she seemed far away. Which meant she was barely speaking at all.

It was sort of like living in a haunted house, except without any actual ghosts.

So when sixth grade finally ended in the middle of June, and Dad invited me for another visit, I said yes right away, even though I knew Mom had argued with Dad about the timing. She'd shut her bedroom door for privacy, but I could hear her loud-but-trying-not-to-shout side of the phone fight: "Ren has her own stuff going on! . . . I don't know—things with her friend Annika this summer, and some other girls in her class! . . . At the town pool! She has a social life, Peter, and you can't just yank her away whenever you want—"

But, Mom, I'm fine being yanked away, I protested in my head. *I don't even want to hang out with Annika. At the pool, or anywhere else.*

In the end Mom agreed to the visit. I flew back to Brooklyn just in time to watch the Fourth of July fireworks from the roof of Vanessa's brownstone.

"Isn't this spectacular," Dad kept saying. "Isn't this the best." Then he'd rub Vanessa's basketball-shaped belly.

A part of me really wanted to hate the whole thing—the booming noises, the chrysanthemum-shaped explosions, Vanessa's belly—but after the spooky quiet of the last few months, the truth was I couldn't stop smiling.

The morning after the fireworks, when I came downstairs for breakfast, Vanessa was sitting at the kitchen island, staring at her laptop. I peeked over her shoulder; she was watching one of those how-to videos.

The topic was makeup.

"Why are you watching that?" I asked as I chomped on my favorite breakfast: an almost-burnt bagel covered in too much extra-crunchy peanut butter.

She seemed embarrassed. "Oh, good morning, Ren. I'm just thinking about makeup for the wedding. But I hardly ever wear any, and I'm kind of an ignoramus when it comes to these things, so I thought maybe if I watched a tutorial—"

"What kind of makeup do you want?"

"I'm not sure." She gave a little laugh. "Maybe a cat eye? Nothing too flashy. I like doing art, but I'm not really a makeup person."

I just nodded. Vanessa had never told me she was responsible for the two bad paintings in my room. But by this time I'd figured that out, and I was glad I hadn't made fun of them.

Now she turned her laptop so I had a better angle. On the monitor a woman with a heart-shaped face and magenta lipstick was demonstrating how to use eyeliner: "Make your wing drawing a line with black eye pencil, starting from the last lash outward. Draw a line back to your upper lash line, creating an empty triangle on your upper lid. Then fill in with liquid eyeliner."

Vanessa groaned. "Impossible, right?"

"Actually, I think it looks pretty simple," I said. "Do you have any of that stuff she's using? The pencil and the eyeliner?"

"Yeah, a few days ago I bought out Sephora! But I'm still hopeless at putting it on. Even though I've been practicing."

I had the squirmy feeling again that I couldn't hate Vanessa, even if I wanted to.

"Let me try." I immediately scolded myself: *Are you crazy? You don't know anything about makeup!*

But Vanessa ran upstairs to her bathroom and came back to the kitchen with a small shopping bag stuffed with supplies, and a hand mirror. "I was thinking of hiring a professional makeup person, but I want a very simple look, and I'm afraid they'll overdo it. Please use just a little," she said, almost like she was apologizing.

"You hardly need any, to be honest," I said. And before I could let myself think, or get nervous, I applied the black pencil, then the eyeliner.

A few quick strokes, nothing to it. Cat eye.

"That's perfect!" Vanessa exclaimed as she looked at herself in the mirror. "Oh, Ren, I love it! You're really a much better artist than I am!"

I was blushing. "No, I'm not. I just followed the directions."

"Seriously, though, it's *exactly* what I wanted! Would you do this for the wedding? Please?"

"Sure," I said. Then, because I was feeling brave, I asked if I could watch a video that was due up next in her feed: *Catwoman Makeup by Cat FX.*

Because: whoa. Someone could teach you how to look like Catwoman? That was something you could actually *learn*?

"Watch all you like," Vanessa told me as she stared at herself in the mirror.

Good Weird

That's how the whole thing started.

I watched Cat FX's Catwoman video, then her Shuri video, then her Nebula. I watched each of them like three or four times.

The incredible part, which I couldn't get enough of, was how Cat FX transformed herself. At the start of every video she'd talk to you without any makeup, the way she looked in real life. Not as old as Mom or Vanessa, not as young as me. Not ugly, not pretty, just a regular face with slightly puffy brown eyes, snub nose, blotchy pale skin, stringy blond hair. The kind of person who wore baggy sweaters, whose scruffy dog you'd pet if they passed you on the street.

"Hey, guys." She always greeted you with a froggy morning voice, waving both hands at the camera. "Cat FX here. Sorry if I look weird this morning, but I hardly got a wink of sleep last night. *Not a wink.* Isn't that a strange expression? Because who winks in their sleep? And if you did wink, your other eye would be open, so you wouldn't actually be sleeping, right?"

Or she'd tell you about a car-chase dream she'd had. Or apologize for having a cold. Or for not drinking enough coffee before recording.

"Hey, guys, Cat FX here. We got our first snow this morning, so I'm, like, celebrating."

"Hey, guys. It's me again. Sorry if I seem distracted—I think my phone died last night."

"Hey, guys. So does anyone know what to do if your cat keeps barfing hairballs? I swear, Beelzebub is doing it on purpose, just to be evil."

You know—normal-person stuff like that.

But then, little by little, step by step, she'd start transforming herself into different fantasy creatures: monsters, superheroes, cyborgs, fairies. Mermaids—but not the babyish kind. The kind that seemed like alien sea creatures.

"Don't be afraid to explore the weirdness of these characters," Cat FX would say as she was applying Elmer's glue to her eyebrows. "Because here's my secret message: There's good weird and bad weird. Bad weird is negative and based on hate; I never do bad weird with my makeup, *ever.* But good weird? That's pretty much the point of all this, guys. Because good weird tells the world who you really are."

I watched more Cat FX videos the next day, and the day after that. She'd done a million of them over two years, and I couldn't stop watching. I took one break to go up on the brownstone roof to grill some hot dogs with Dad—and that was it. I even watched on my phone in the middle of the night when I couldn't sleep.

Cat FX's videos weren't the only ones I checked out online. I also watched other makeup artists with names like PrincessTinkRbelle and Alienne and She-Wolf23. But the best one was definitely Cat FX. There was something about the way she explained what she was doing—her "technique," she called it—that just made sense somehow. Like, if you're doing Evil Snowman makeup, *of course* you want to use liquid latex before you apply white face paint, followed by black eye shadow. *Of course* that's the correct order.

And it was almost like she was speaking directly to me: *Okay, Ren-who-hates-the-name-Renata, I know that everything is crazy for you right now: You have no control over your parents, or your home, or your social life, or anything else, for that matter. But if you have the right eyeliner, and the right* foundation, and if you use the right brushes—Cat FX was very big on brushes—*you can transform yourself completely.*

You can be this powerful, mysterious creature. A superhero, an alien, or anything else you can imagine.

And you can make up your own storyline. Your own back-story, too. Your superpowers (if you have any). Also your weaknesses, dreams, secrets, allies, and enemies.

Good weird. The opposite of bad weird.

Watching videos for three days straight made me realize all the stuff I needed—way more than Vanessa's little shopping bag of supplies. So when Vanessa suggested taking me shopping for a dress to wear at the wedding, I asked if we could go makeup shopping too.

She seemed unsure. "Is this about those YouTube videos?"

"Yeah," I admitted. "Don't worry—I won't wear any of it to your wedding. Or to school. It's just sort of a research project."

She agreed to take me. Maybe she liked the words "research project." Or maybe as a painter she understood about art supplies. Or maybe she thought this was her chance to be Cool Stepmom.

I didn't tell Mom about the makeup when I got home two days later. I guess I felt guilty for letting Vanessa buy me stuff, especially expensive products. And anyhow,

Mom was busy with work—sleeping as soon as she got home from the hospital, dealing with her sore back and bad knee.

Plus, with the wedding coming up just next month, and the babies coming soon after that, I didn't want to upset her any worse.

Evil Zombie

Hey, guys. Cat FX here. Sorry if I seem a little out of it this morning. Beelzebub kept howling at the moon or something. I hate him forever now. Not really.

Anyway. Enough about me.

So here's today's secret formula for great makeup effects: Be bold! Commit to the look! Use deep pigments, black eyeliner, and sparkles. But— and I hope you're listening closely to this, guys—don't do everything all at once! Make choices: a dramatic eye, a strong mouth, a great wig. Wherever you're going, choose two or three elements to develop to the max, or you'll undermine the impact.

And the most important thing: Unleash your imagination! Take risks and have fun!

o O o

Annika had been my sort-of-friend since the start of sixth grade, even though I could never figure out why. Everything I did, she made some snotty comment about—like, *Omigod, I can't believe you just said that.* Or: *Oh, Ren, you're sooo weee-ird.* And by "weird" I was pretty sure she meant bad weird.

But everyone wanted to be friends with Annika, so I felt lucky that she'd picked me. Not because I liked *her*, but because I didn't want her for an enemy. She was the kind of popular that was based on meanness—giving nasty nicknames, spreading lies and gossip about kids she didn't like. And, because I needed to not think too hard about Annika, I told myself that it was okay to be friends with her as long as *I* wasn't being mean.

About a week after I got back from New York, Annika invited me to a "makeup party." Whatever Mom had told Dad about my "social life," I actually had nothing on my calendar that summer except going to the town pool with Annika and her other friends. But I knew if I said no to this invitation, I'd never be invited—possibly to anything—ever again.

The party was in Annika's bedroom. She'd invited two other girls from the lunch table, Raleigh and Isla, who'd brought a few things with them in sandwich bags— mascara, lip gloss, nail polish, blush. From my shopping trip with Vanessa, I now had a small shopping bag's worth of supplies, which I'd slipped inside my backpack.

When I unzipped my backpack to spread out my stuff on Annika's bed, everybody gasped.

"Omigod, Ren, where did you get all that?" Raleigh asked.

"My almost-stepmom took me shopping," I said. "I'm doing her makeup for the wedding, so this was a thank-you present."

"You're doing her *wedding makeup*?" Annika's pale blue eyes were bugging.

I shrugged. "Yeah, I've been watching a ton of YouTube videos. Makeup is kind of an obsession for me lately."

I knew this was bragging. But seeing Annika's jealous expression—and the way she couldn't come up with a snide remark for once—made it worth it.

"Whoa," Isla said. She picked up the little plastic case that held the false eyelashes. "Can I use these?"

"Ren, could you do my makeup? Pleeeease?" Raleigh begged.

"Do me," Annika said. "Anyhow, it's my party."

"Nah." I flicked my hand. "You wouldn't like the kind of makeup I'm into."

Annika snorted. "How do you know *that*?"

"Because I don't do regular makeup. Only special effects."

"*Special effects?*" Annika pressed her lips at me. "You know what *I* think, Ren? I think you just don't want to share your stuff. And you only brought it over here to show off."

"That's not true," I protested. But immediately I wondered: *Why did I bring it, anyway?*

"So do me, then," Annika said in an *I dare you* sort of voice. "If you're so great at it, Renahhh-tahhh."

The way she said it made me hate my name even worse.

"Unless you're scared," she added, smirking.

That was it. All the times I'd looked away when Annika was nasty, all the times I could have—should have—spoken up came whooshing into my brain. And before I could think about it, I decided what to do.

"Fine," I told Annika. "Except no mirrors. You have to let me do your makeup without watching, or I'll get nervous. And Raleigh and Isla can watch, but they can't say anything while I'm working."

I got halfway through Evil Zombie when Raleigh and Isla covered their mouths, giggling.

And then Annika jumped up from the chair, ran to her bathroom mirror, and screamed.

Bride of Frankenstein

Mom looked worried as she drove me home a half hour later. Annika's mom had called her at the hospital, so she'd had to leave work to come get me.

"Ren, what came over you?" she asked. "Annika's mom is very upset. Did you actually think Annika *wanted* to look like a zombie?"

"Well, maybe not," I admitted. "But she kind of forced me into it."

"She *forced* you?"

"She made me feel like I had to do *something*. To show her how I felt. About a lot of things."

"Hmm," Mom said. She drove without talking. Then she said, "Annika's not much of a friend, is she."

"Not really. Although she's mean to a lot of people, not just me."

"Have you ever tried talking to her? Telling her how you feel? Before this makeup business, I mean."

I shrugged.

"Ren, it's really important to share your feelings, you know? Because if you don't, they have a way of coming back to bite you in the butt."

It was strange to hear Mom say that when she couldn't even say the word "divorce." But I smiled at that expression: *bite you in the butt.*

"I'll try," I said. And then, out of relief that Mom understood about Annika, I kept going. "Anyhow, I told her I only did special makeup effects, like they do for movies. But she wouldn't listen."

Mom took her eyes off the road to stare at me. "You do *movie makeup*? Ren, what are you talking about?"

"I mean, I'm just learning," I said quickly. "*Trying* to learn. There's like a million makeup artists doing tutorials on YouTube. I've watched a ton of them by now. But my favorite is this one named Cat FX. She explains all these amazing techniques step-by-step. Like how to do zombies and mermaids and superheroes—"

"Wow. I didn't know. When did this start?"

"It just did, actually. In Brooklyn."

"Oh, *Brooklyn*." Mom said the name like it tasted funny in her mouth. "Can I ask you a question, Ren? Where did you get all that makeup you put on Annika? From Vanessa?"

"Yeah. She took me shopping. It was really nice of her," I added quickly. "Some of it's pretty expensive, so."

Mom sighed. "You know, Ren, if you need things, you should be asking *me*. I may not have as much money to spend as Vanessa—"

Ugh. "Sorry," I said.

"—but I can take you shopping too. Also, if you have a new hobby, you should tell me about it. Not just Vanessa. Or your father."

"I know," I said in a small voice. "You're right. I'm really sorry."

"Okay." Mom drove a few blocks without talking. She was upset with me, and for a good reason. Why had I asked Vanessa to buy me stuff, and basically in secret? Why hadn't I told Mom about the makeup videos? I was selfish and stupid. Not to mention unfair to Mom, who understood about Annika, and wasn't even mad for having to leave work to come rescue me.

But all of a sudden Mom said, "Hey, you know what would be cool? Could you make me Bride of Frankenstein?"

I looked at her. "I'm not sure. Is that monster makeup?"

She snorted. "You're studying movie makeup and you don't know Bride of Frankenstein?"

"Not yet. Mom, I'm just getting started!"

"Hmph," Mom said. "It's a makeup classic. Well, when we get home, you and I are watching that movie."

That night was the first time I ever did Mom's makeup. I was nervous, because except for Vanessa's cat eyes, and the zombie I did on Annika, I'd only ever done makeup effects on myself. And even though my face wasn't what you'd call interesting—my eyes were too small, my cheeks were pale and too round, my hair was straight and boring brown—I felt safe just working on my own features. Especially if I smudged the eyeliner, used the wrong foundation, spilled silver glitter all over the table, or whatever.

And don't go, *Oh, come on, it's just your mom, the person who loves you no matter what, so why be nervous?* The thing was, I really cared about Mom's opinion. I wanted her to think I was *actually good* at this. Plus, Bride of Franken-stein was complicated, with those weird pointy eyebrows and all the scars. But incredibly fun to do, even if we didn't have the crazy electric-shock wig—and the best part was seeing Mom happy, better than she'd been since Dad left.

When the makeup was finally done, she called me "brilliant and talented."

"Now I *insist* you take a close-up, dahling," she said in a Hollywood diva voice. "And send it to Dad," she added, wink-ing. But I was sure that was a joke.

Wren

After the makeup party, Annika stopped talking to me. Of course, that meant Isla and Raleigh had to stop talking to me too. But they went blabbing to everybody else that I'd tricked Annika into looking like a zombie. At her own party, in her own house. Just to humiliate her in front of her friends.

By the middle of the summer, I was hazardous-waste material, off-limits to everyone going into seventh grade. You couldn't have a conversation with me at the pool without Annika finding out about it, and being furious at you for "taking sides" against her. Not that I had a side—or that I was even "against" Annika. But since nobody wanted to deal with *her*, they just avoided *me*. I swam by myself for about a week, watched some videos on my phone over by the ice cream truck, and then just stopped going to the pool completely.

It's fine, I told myself. *More time to practice my makeup. Create new characters or whatever.*

I'm not even lonely.

And when it was time for Dad and Vanessa's wedding, I was relieved to escape Abingdon. The wedding was small—just Grandma Ellen, Vanessa's brother and his family, a few of Vanessa's friends, somebody's toddler, the photographer, and me. It happened in the middle of August, on a beach somewhere in Connecticut. A quick ceremony, but long enough that after a minute or two you could taste seawater, and feel the grit of wet sand between your toes, even if you were wearing sandals.

Vanessa wore a big swishy wedding gown that billowed around her huge belly. Her face had hardly any makeup, but she didn't forget to ask me to do her eyes. For a second I thought it might be funny to give her a Catwoman sort of effect, with a big dramatic wing and purple eye shadow. But of course I wouldn't do that to her the way I did to Annika. Not on her wedding, not ever. Vanessa was too nice for that, really.

After the ceremony, she kissed my cheek. "Thank you, Ren, for making me feel beautiful today."

Dad whispered in my ear, "Vanessa loves you, jellybean. And you know I do, right?"

"I love you too, Dad."

His eyes got all red and swimmy. Then he took my hand and held it between his big ones. *A hand sandwich:* our family's thing since I was little, when I thought it was the funniest joke ever.

I flew home to Abingdon the next morning. Mom acted like I'd been away on a school trip, or at a sleepover. She didn't want wedding details: that was obvious. So I didn't share the photos Vanessa sent me, not even the one of me wading into the ocean, the wind tossing my hair in a million directions, like I was a mermaid going home after visiting the seashore.

A few days after the wedding, I was in the kitchen eating some microwaved spaghetti for dinner when Mom sat down across from me. The night before she'd let me do another character on her: Creepy Broken Doll. But now, without any makeup at all—no under-eye concealer, no foundation—her skin looked kind of like leftover oatmeal. Not the sort of warm golden brown she usually was by this time of the summer.

And it was weird how she was just sitting there, watching me twirl the spaghetti on my fork. Not saying a word.

"You want some?" I asked after about a minute.

She shook her head. "I'll eat later."

"How come you never eat with me anymore?"

"Because my work schedule keeps getting changed! It's thrown off everything—my sleep, my appetite. It's like my body is confused." Her forehead scrunched. "Hey, honeybee, can we talk?"

I put down my fork. *Uh-oh, now what?*

"Ren, I've been thinking," Mom said. "This house is too big for just the two of us, my hospital supervisor hates me, and you don't have any friends here—not good ones. So what if we moved?"

"Wait, what?" My jaw literally dropped. "You mean leave Abingdon? And your job? And my school?"

"We're both unhappy here, aren't we? I know it's been really hard for you lately. The way Annika's turned everyone against you."

How did Mom even know that? I'd never told her about Raleigh and Isla blabbing. Or what it was like for me at the pool. It was like Mom had telepathy about me or something, and I suddenly felt relieved she knew the truth. But even so, hearing those words—*Annika's turned everyone against you*—made my eyes sting.

"I don't care about Annika," I told her. "She's nothing but mean. I'm actually glad we're not friends anymore!"

"Well, she's totally wrecked your social life! All you do is sit in your room by yourself watching makeup videos. I'm worried about you."

"But why? I *love* watching makeup videos! They're fascinating!"

"I'm not saying they aren't, Rennie. But you should have other things going on too. Other activities, and more friends."

I pushed away my plate. "Fine, I'll get more friends. When seventh grade starts."

"Sweetheart, you need a change. We both do." Mom's fingers were shredding a napkin while she talked. "This town is just not working for us anymore. I'm tired of answering questions about your father's whereabouts. And sick of proving myself to a supervisor who doesn't trust me."

So this was about her, not me. And not about Annika's meanness, or the pool, or the makeup party. "Why doesn't your supervisor trust you?"

"It's a long story."

"Tell me." I crossed my arms.

In some ways Mom and I were alike: Most of the time we hated fighting, but when something mattered, we could be stubborn. So I guess it was obvious I wouldn't let her get away without answering.

She took a second, raking her fingers through her too-long bangs.

"All right," she said. "So what happened was, I made one stupid mistake with a patient's meds. I was tired, and

I may have miscalculated a little; a few pills went missing. This kind of thing happens in hospitals *all the time*, and the patient was *fine*, but now the supervisor is breathing down my neck, watching me every second, and it's driving me crazy. The point is, we could both use a fresh start."

"But where? We can't just pick up and—"

"Actually, we can. I got a job offer from another hospital. In Donwood."

I swallowed. "Where's that?"

"A town about fifty miles from here. I can rent out this house with all our furniture, and I've already put a security deposit on a small townhouse."

"Wait, you have? What's a townhouse?"

"Like an apartment with two floors. It's really nice: they allow pets, you'll have a good-sized bedroom, and the kitchen is sunny. The landlord says we can move in August thirty-first. So you'll have more than a week to settle in before school starts."

"But, Mom." I couldn't even think of other words to add to that sentence. My head was spinning. *More changes? How many more could there be?*

"Hand sandwich," Mom said, reaching across the table to take my hand between hers. "You know, honeybee, your father got to make his choice, and I get to make a choice too. It's only fair." Her eyes filled. "Please just trust me on this, okay, Rennie? I really think this move is going to be great."

I didn't answer.

Because I knew she wasn't asking for permission. And anyway, she didn't need it. She could do whatever she wanted. Both my parents could. Both my parents *did*.

But maybe there was something I could choose also. An idea that my brain couldn't let go of, one change that was tiny but still important.

Because it showed who I really was, deep inside. Kind of like a makeup effect without the makeup.

Later that night I squished next to Mom on the sofa. She was watching some detective series with the sound so low you could barely hear it. On the table in front of her was her red mug, half full of milky tea.

"I've decided I'm okay about moving," I announced. "And since we are, I have to tell you something I've been thinking about a lot lately. I want to change my name."

"I'm sorry, what?" Mom said. She seemed lost in thought, like she hadn't even been paying attention to her show.

I spoke very fast. "I've never felt like a *Renata Lewis*. I always hate it when people call me that, so from now on I want everyone to call me Wren. Pronounced the same as Ren, but with a silent *W*."

Mom clicked off the remote. "Sweetheart, what sense does it make to add a silent letter? Wren sounds exactly the same as Ren—"

"Except it's different," I insisted. "Wrens are tiny little songbirds, but they're fierce. They can fight much bigger birds when they have to; I looked it up online. And as long as we're moving, it's the perfect time to make the switch. A fresh start, like you said."

"Oh, honeybee," Mom said. She seemed sad. "Renata is a beautiful name your father and I picked for you."

I shrugged. "I know. I just want to pick a name for myself."

"That's not how names work." Mom rubbed her forehead like she was trying to erase something. "But change can be important. I get that. I do."

"Thank you." I threw my arms around her. Because Mom really did get it. And me, actually.

She sighed deeply and kissed my hair. *"Wren,"* she said, pronouncing the silent *W*.

Nebula

You know what I love best about special-effects makeup? When you look at yourself in the mirror and go: Hey, is that me? And then you answer: Yes, it is! The real me. Because here's my secret message to you guys: fantasy is not the opposite of truth.

Somehow Mom managed it that two weeks later, the four of us—her, me, Lulu, and Cyrus—were in the new townhouse. She seemed electrified, like she'd been zapped by lightning. We painted the kitchen a pale green color called Midmorning Rain, bleached the tiles in both bathrooms (she insisted the previous family had left behind germs), and hung white curtains on all the windows. While we worked, she even played Spotify on her phone and sang along—loudly, and a little off-key—to her favorite old music.

And what it all boils down to
Is that no one's really got it figured out just yet
Well, I've got one hand in my pocket
And the other one is playing a piano.

Alanis Morissette's music wasn't exactly happy, but Mom kept smiling as she de-germed our new kitchen. And I had to admit she was right—this small house was the right size for two people with two not-very-large, not-very-active pets. I also liked that we didn't have the old furniture, just some stuff we'd bought at the Donwood Target.

It felt like a new beginning for us both. Not just some new chairs and tables, but also a new job for Mom. A new school—and a new name—for me.

Another thing Mom had been right about—I'd been lonely. I guess sometimes when you're stuck in the middle of something, you stop seeing it the way it really is. Or you focus on one teeny detail, but you don't see the whole big picture. And I think back in Abingdon I'd been so focused on all the parent stuff, and on my "hobby" (to use Mom's word), that I hadn't noticed how little I spoke to people, how often I was by myself, in my room.

But when seventh grade started at Donwood Middle School, it was like I was a new toy in the toy box, and people were curious how I worked. Kids sat with me in the lunchroom, asking all sorts of questions. Where did I live before? What was my old school like? Did I play any sports? I knew that soon enough they'd decide my interests were weird, that I was awkward and not-sporty and too quiet. But for the first couple of weeks, anyway, the attention felt good, like warm sunshine after a snowy winter.

Also, it was cool just seeing new faces, trying to figure out who was friends with who, who was snobby, who was shy, who was possibly a genius at something. Studying their eyes, the way they smiled, how they bit their nails or flipped their hair.

And then my brain started going: *That kid Mateo has a jawline almost like Timothée Chalamet's.*

Camila's cheeks would look great with blue highlighter.

Kai is always by himself. I wonder why his hair sticks up like that. And am I imagining it, or are his eyes two different colors?

One time toward the end of September I was doodling a cybernetic eye on my math worksheet when a tall, strong-looking white girl with a million freckles and dark-reddish hair snatched the paper right off my desk. I'd noticed her before: she had the old-timey Hollywood name Poppy Fairbanks, and mostly hung out with athlete kids and drama kids. Although, really, she was popular with the whole seventh grade—but not mean popular, like Annika.

Nice popular, because she talked to everybody and had a laugh that reminded me of a waterfall.

But when she snatched the drawing, my first reaction was panic. Was she going to laugh at *me*?

Instead she gasped.

"Oh. My. God," she said. "This. Is. Amazing."

"No, not really," I said. "It's just a sketch—"

"Of what?"

"Nebula." I made *not so loud* hands. "I'm learning special-effects makeup. *Trying* to learn. It's really hard to get the details right, though, especially with the cybernetic eye. You need to make it look like machine parts—"

She stared at my drawing. "You're a *makeup artist*?"

My cheeks burned. "No, no! I've just been watching a lot of how-to videos. And practicing. There are all these special techniques—"

Suddenly the boy named Kai lurched forward, grabbing his worksheet just before it sailed off his desk. Some kids behind him sniggered.

Poppy ignored the whole thing. "Hey, look at this!" She grabbed Avery's sleeve. "Wren is a makeup artist! And she's doing Nebula!"

"Who?"

"You know, the superhero. From the Avengers."

Avery, a tiny, pretty Black girl with a half bun, glanced

at the drawing. All I knew about her was that she'd been the star of every play since preschool. For the first week of school she'd talked to me a little, like she was giving me an audition. Which I'd failed, apparently; now she said hello when we passed each other in the hall, but that was it.

"Nice," she said. Her smile flickered like an old light bulb.

I watched her whisper something to Minna, whose thick, wavy brown hair almost—but not really—hid a brace that reached up to her neck.

Avery and Minna were obviously not interested in my drawing. Neither was Camila, a smiley girl who was showing Mateo something on her phone. Or Kai, whose possibly mismatched eyes met mine before he hunched over his worksheet.

Poppy didn't care that we were distracting Kai and the other kids sitting nearby. She just kept gushing. "Wren, you're so talented! I wish I could draw like that! Or do superhero effects, or whatever you call it! Could you show me how?"

Then I did something crazy. I mean, not like myself at all.

Maybe it had to do with being Wren now—a small change but also a big one.

"Actually," I said quietly, "you know what would be great? If I could practice on you sometime. I mean, if you want."

She gaped. "Practice on *me*? You mean give me *super-hero makeup*?"

"Although you'd have to sit still," I added. "And not change your expression while I work. It can be extremely boring—"

"Are you *serious*?" Poppy waved my drawing like a flag. "How could it be boring to look like *this*?"

"Girls, enough consultation," Ms. Arroyo, the math teacher, warned from the other side of the classroom. "Class ends in three minutes."

"Are you busy after school?" Poppy whispered. "I do soccer most afternoons, but I'm free today."

"Today would be great," I said. My brain raced. Mom had a shift at the hospital that ended at five, but she often stayed afterward "to finish up," whatever that meant.

So if Poppy came to our house straight after school, that would give us about two and a half hours, which was definitely enough time to try the pigment Vanessa had sent me last week. Vanessa had had it mailed straight from the makeup company, so her name wasn't on the envelope's return address. Did Vanessa do it this way so Mom wouldn't know it was from her? I couldn't help wondering.

Anyhow, I told myself, *it's just a small jar of pigment. Not worth upsetting Mom about.*

The Net

For beginners, I always suggest using your own face as your model. Doing makeup on yourself is the best way to build confidence in your technique.

But after a while, it's so important to practice on other faces. You need to work with all kinds of skin tones, eyebrows, noses, and chins. Not just your own every time.

So here's my secret message: Don't be shy! The more you include other people in your work, the more you'll develop as a makeup artist.

That's how my friendship with Poppy began. I think she liked me because I was new and different—not another soccer kid or drama kid. I think she was curious about all the makeup—especially the fancy special-effects stuff

Vanessa had been sending, which I'd been hiding in a shoe-box labeled *V*, so that Mom wouldn't know. But also the things I kept in a shoebox marked *M*: the stuff Mom bought for me, which I needed to keep separate.

And I think Poppy liked coming over because (except for Lulu and Cyrus) our house was usually empty after school. Versus Poppy's house, which had an annoying little sister and a high school brother who played video games with the volume turned way up. Also a mom who kept calling from work every twenty minutes to "check in" about doing homework.

Plus, our kitchen shelves were full of snacks. The nurses' break room at the hospital had piles of chips and cookies in little packets, and every time Mom had a shift, she'd grab a handful to bring home.

"This stuff doesn't seem very nursey," Poppy commented the third time she came over, as she nibbled a packet of Chips Ahoy. "I mean, you'd think they'd all be eating carrot sticks."

"Actually, nurses eat a ton of junk food," I said. "Especially on the night shift. For stress."

"Your mom works night shifts?"

"Sometimes. Yeah."

"Don't you mind when she does? Being home all by yourself?"

"Nah, I'm used to it." I explained how Dad used to be home for Mom's night shifts, unless he was traveling. And when he left our house to live with Vanessa, Mom insisted I needed a babysitter—"a companion," she'd called it. But I'd insisted I was too old, and finally she gave up.

"Whoa," Poppy said. "That's amazing, Wren. I never win fights with *my* mom."

I shrugged. "Well, it wasn't a *fight*. My mom and I don't really fight about things."

"You *don't*? Seriously?" Poppy laughed. "That's actually kind of weird."

The word "weird" had an almost Annika sound to it, and I flinched. But then I checked Poppy's face: Her eyes were bright and kind. No meanness, no judging.

Good weird.

I smiled back at her.

After our snacks Poppy and I went upstairs to my bedroom. The first time we did makeup, she insisted on Nebula, exactly according to Cat FX's instructions. But when I showed her the latest supplies Vanessa had sent me, she asked if we could try something not so superheroic. More like real life, she said—maybe Person with a Bad Cold. Or Person with a Black Eye. Or Person with an Allergic Reaction.

"Allergic to what, specifically?" I said. "Because if it's pollen, it'll look exactly like Bad Cold. Puffy eyes, pink nose—"

"Yeah, I guess." Poppy's face lit up. "Or wait—how about Poison Ivy Rash!"

"Cat FX doesn't do rashes," I said, making an *ew* face. "None of the makeup artists I follow do."

"Okay, so you be the first! Oh, come on, Wren, *pleeeease*?"

How could I say no? And I had to admit the first few poison ivy blisters were fun, all pink and oozy. But after a while they got boring—because, really, how many different kinds of blisters could you make? Poppy was ecstatic with how it turned out, though; she couldn't stop laughing when I took her photo.

The next time, we did Frostbite—tricky, because according to Cat FX's Evil Snowman video, you needed white cream makeup (which I didn't have) and a stipple brush (which ditto). So instead I used a ton of too-light face powder on Poppy, highlighting with shades of blue and purple. I also used liquid latex (which I had, thanks to Vanessa) and rolled-up bits of tissue to make icicles dripping from Poppy's eyebrows, nose, and chin.

Then Poppy suggested Too Much Plastic Surgery. This one sounded fun, but after a few minutes I knew it was too advanced. To do it right, you needed to make prosthetics—a fake pinched nose, puffy lips, and a too-high, too-smooth forehead—and I wasn't ready for that step yet. So I just did Too Much Makeup, giving Poppy a face that looked like melted crayons.

When I finished, Poppy thought it was so hilarious she made me take a photo to send to Avery and Minna. I tried to tell her it wasn't very good, but she just laughed and said I was crazy.

Not in an *Oh, Wren, you're sooo weeeird* sort of way, like Annika. More like: *You're really talented at this, Wren. Don't be so modest.*

Only Mom had ever made me feel this proud of my work. So I didn't argue.

The week after that we started working on mermaid makeup. Poppy was a good person to practice on because she could hold very still, even though she talked a lot. And she never argued when I suggested something crazy.

For example, putting a fishnet stocking over her head. I'd seen Cat FX do it in the mermaid video—you very lightly brushed green and silver pigment over the netting to make it look like scales. I still wasn't getting the irides- cent effect, though—and I was wondering why when Poppy startled me.

"Sooo," she said, "here's a burning question for you, Wren. Do you *like* anyone?"

"What do you mean?" I said.

"I mean any boys at school. Or girls," she added, glancing at my face in the mirror.

"I don't know," I said. "I mean, I just moved here."

"Not true! You've been here more than a month!"

"Yeah, but I'm still just noticing people." For example, Mateo with his sharp jawline. Avery with her eyes that were always judging. Minna with her hair not hiding her brace. And Kai, who chewed his nails, barely spoke to anyone, and kept comics hidden under his desk. "Anyhow, I don't get crushes just by noticing," I added.

"Really? How *do* you get crushes, then?"

Good question. Because I'm not sure I've ever had one, truthfully. "It's hard to describe."

"Well, *I* can just look at someone and wham. Instant crush." Poppy laughed her waterfall laugh. "Wanna know who I like right now? Emmett Brooker."

"Who?"

"In our math class? And also in Spanish? And he sits by the window in ELA?"

"Oh yeah," I said. "Him." Emmett was sort of the boy version of Poppy: outgoing, nice-popular. A tall Black kid with a lopsided smile. He'd chatted with me the first week or so, then stopped. But not in a mean way, more like he just ran out of conversation.

"Avery likes him too," Poppy continued. "He's an amazing singer. Can I tell you something? She's desperate to play Elphaba, and I'm sure she'll get it, because she's super talented. And she wants Emmett to play Fiyero, so they can sing 'As Long As You're Mine' together."

"What's that?"

"The big love duet in *Wicked*!" When I didn't say anything, Poppy groaned. "This year's spring musical? Come on, Wren, you *have* to know about this! There are posters up *all over school*!"

"Oh right," I said, concentrating hard as I lightly brushed her cheek with some blue eye shadow. All I knew about *Wicked* was that it was based on *The Wizard of Oz*. And that it was about Elphaba, the green-faced Wicked Witch of the West, and her sort-of friendship with perfect, popular Glinda.

"I think I saw those posters," I added. "I mean, I'm pretty sure I did."

"The whole grade's obsessed!" Poppy started wiggling in the chair. "Ms. Belfonte is directing, and she's the best! And I don't know *anyone* who's not trying out. Except the weird kids, like Kai."

I didn't answer. If I told her I couldn't sing or dance, that I had no interest in being onstage, would that make me a weird kid? Probably yes—and *bad* weird too.

I think Poppy could tell I was getting uncomfortable, so she gave me an encouraging sort of smile. "Okay, but seriously, Wren, you *are* doing *Wicked*, right? You *have* to—if you don't, I'll never see you after school! At least be in the chorus." Suddenly her eyes got huge as she grabbed my elbow. "Or, wait—I know! *You could do makeup!*"

"Me?"

Just the thought of it made my stomach twist. Sitting so close to kids I barely knew, telling them not to move, not to breathe.

And what if I messed up? I was still a beginner, not ready for people to judge my work. Plus, I couldn't stop thinking about Annika, how she'd freaked when I turned her into Evil Zombie. I definitely didn't want to go through all that stuff again, with people mad that I didn't make them cute or glamorous.

But other than the fact that Mom was so much happier these days, Poppy was the best thing about moving to Donwood. So I didn't want her to see me as bad weird.

"Okay, I'll think about it," I said as very, very carefully I removed the stocking net from Poppy's head.

The Red Mug

In the last few weeks of Vanessa's pregnancy, she didn't get out much. But she still kept ordering me stuff online—eye-shadow palettes, lipsticks, fancy brushes. Guessing how Mom would react to these packages (not well), I always checked our mailbox the second I got home from school. So "checking the mailbox" became one of my after-school chores, along with emptying the dishwasher and taking Lulu outside for a short walk.

And every time there was a package, I told myself: *It's not like I'm hiding this from Mom to be sneaky. It's just so I don't hurt her feelings.*

Because with Vanessa's due date almost here, I knew Mom was extra sensitive, snippy when I asked about things like her work schedule, which kept changing all the time, it seemed. Sometimes she worked like four late shifts in a row, and then added a full weekend of overtime. Or she'd have a normal week, but stay late "to finish up."

"Finish what up?" I asked her once.

"Charts," she snapped. "Mountains of paperwork, Wren! What do you *think* I'm doing at the hospital after my shift ends?"

I was so surprised by her reaction, I couldn't answer.

An hour later she apologized, explaining that she was upset because one of her patients "didn't make it." I told her I understood, and we hugged, and then she went into her bedroom and shut the door.

When the twins—Ayla and Paxton—finally arrived the second week of October, Dad called to say they'd be fine, but right now they were too tiny to leave the hospital.

"Twins are often underweight at birth, nothing to worry about," Mom told me. She sounded confident, like a nurse on duty. Although right away she changed the subject, so I knew I shouldn't talk about them, or share the sleeping-baby photos Dad kept sending me.

Suddenly my family was feeling bigger and smaller at the same time.

The twins stayed in the hospital for eleven days. Vanessa kept texting me updates: Ayla's numbers are so much better! Paxton gained another ounce!! Always good news, but it was still hard not to worry. And hard not to share all that worry with Mom.

The first weekend the babies were home from the hospital, I flew out to Brooklyn to meet them. To be honest, I didn't care one bit that this meant missing Poppy's Halloween party. And even though all the babies did was sleep, eat, cry, and pee, I loved how their hair smelled like lotion and sunshine, and how they gripped my pinky in their tiny, red, wrinkled hands.

The whole time I was in New York, Dad kept taking photos. Me with Paxton. Me with Ayla. Me with Ayla and Paxton. *My new siblings,* I told myself. But I couldn't help feeling a little bit awkward about them. And then feeling guilty about feeling awkward.

Once when I was sitting on the sofa holding Ayla wrapped in a blanket, Dad snapped our picture and beamed at us.

"Our family is now complete," he said.

Which seemed to me like a funny thing to say.

Because what was it before this?

And what is it when I go back home to Mom?

"Mom?"

She was on the sofa, watching some talk show on TV—but not really watching. Just sort of noticing it with half-closed eyes while Lulu curled around her legs, making old-dog breathing sounds.

And she had the volume so loud it hurt my ears. So I turned it to Mute. "Mom, why aren't you getting ready for work?"

"Why?" Her voice was draggy, like it was on the wrong speed. "What time is it?"

"Three twenty. I just got home. *From school*," I added, because she still didn't seem completely awake. "Didn't you tell me you had a shift tonight?"

"Ugh, that's right." She groaned. "But I have this terrible headache. Maybe I'll ask Krystal to take my shift."

Krystal was another nurse in the ER, the only work friend Mom ever mentioned. I hadn't met her. All I knew about her was that she had two sons: a smart but misbehaving teen named Tyndall and a cute five-year-old named Tucker.

"Well, I'm not surprised you have a headache," I said. "The TV was so loud I could hear it on the street." I rubbed Lulu's ear. "You want a coffee? And a Tylenol?"

"Yes, please. Make that two Tylenols, okay? My head is just *pounding*."

I went to the kitchen. All the breakfast dishes were still in the sink, so while the water was heating for coffee, I washed them and put them in the dish rack to dry. What had Mom been doing all day, anyway?

I hoped it wasn't sleeping again. She didn't seem depressed like she'd been back in Abingdon, when Dad first left us—but the truth was, ever since the babies were born, she'd been too quiet, or else restless and grumpy. And she'd been watching a whole lot of TV lately. Although plenty of people did, even during the day, I told myself as I turned off the faucet. It didn't mean you had a problem—that you were depressed or something.

Besides, Mom's crazy schedule gave her insomnia at night, so it wasn't fair to blame her for being so drowsy during the day.

I brought her the coffee in her special red mug. "Here you go," I said in a cheery voice. "One percent milk, and one teaspoon sugar. Now I'll get you some Tylenol. You have some upstairs?"

"What?" She blinked. "No. Never mind."

"You don't have any Tylenol? In your medicine cabinet? In your bathroom?"

"I said *no!*" Mom shouted. Her face was red. "And can I ask you to *please* stay out of my bathroom? *And* my bedroom?"

Her sudden fierceness shocked me. And, as much as I hated arguing, I had to answer.

"Mom, I never go in your bedroom," I said. "*Or* your bathroom. Why would I? I have my own—"

"Exactly! So it would be nice if you cleaned it once in a while! It may not be as fancy as Vanessa's—"

"Vanessa's bathrooms aren't fancy." I choked back tears. Why was she acting like this?

"—but all those wet, bunched-up towels stink from mildew. Your sink is filthy, Wren; all that makeup stuff leaves stains! And considering how hard I work at the hospital, I'd appreciate a little more help from you around here. If you can pull yourself away from that computer!"

"Sorry," I muttered, just to end the conversation.

Not even looking at me, she got up from the sofa stiffly and hobbled upstairs, leaving the red mug on the coffee table.

The Deal

I was so upset that when Mom left for work a half hour later, I didn't even come out of my room to say goodbye. Why had she attacked me like that, out of nowhere? All I'd done was remind her she had a job. And then wash the dishes, without even being asked. And make coffee, and offer to fetch medicine for her headache.

And that stuff she'd said about Vanessa's bathroom? The truth was, Vanessa's bathrooms *were* pretty fancy, with extra towels in different sizes, and little soaps you weren't supposed to use. But there was no way Mom could even know any of that. She was just *assuming* Vanessa's bathrooms were nicer than hers, probably because she was jealous about the babies.

I mean, it wasn't like I didn't get it. Once, about a couple of years ago, when we were clearing out my old toys from the basement, Mom had told me she'd wanted another baby, a little sibling for me—but "the fertility gods didn't agree." And now Dad had gone off and had *two* babies. So Vanessa's pregnancy, the twins' birth, my visit to see them—all of it must have been really hard for her.

Still. None of that was my fault. Or my choice. So I totally didn't deserve to get scolded. It was just unfair.

And besides, my bathroom was clean and fresh-smelling. All my towels were unbunched and dry. The sink was spotless: no makeup stains anywhere. It was like Mom had imagined the whole thing, or made it up on purpose, just to have an excuse to yell at me. When I'd only been trying to help.

But I knew if I kept thinking about this, I'd go nuts. So I made myself busy—I took Lulu out to pee and did my math homework. Then I checked my makeup supplies. Everything was where it needed to be—in separate shoeboxes, the Mom box and the Vanessa box. I didn't even want to think about what would happen if Mom discovered the makeup supplies from Vanessa.

I pushed the Vanessa box under my bed, into the farthest corner, and watched a bunch of makeup videos, which were extremely educational:

The point of fairy makeup is to accentuate the size of the eyes, so you can't really tell age. Or gender.

If you're wearing a mask, rub Vaseline on your eyebrows so they don't peel off.

To make a unicorn's horn, stack balls of aluminum foil, smear them with latex, let them dry, then paint.

To do Evil Tooth Fairy, rub red food coloring on your lips, extra messy. Get your teeth all red and messy too. This character demands mess and gore, so don't hold back! Have fun with it, guys! Commit to the character!

At seven the garage door grunched open. Mom's shift was supposed to start at five. So this meant she was home extra early.

I heard her clomping up the steps until she reached my bedroom. Then she did a shave-and-a-haircut knock on my closed door.

"Hey, Wren." Mom's voice sounded almost shy. She opened the door just a crack and peeked in. "Can we please talk for a minute?"

"I guess," I said.

She sat on the edge of my bed beside Cyrus, who was curled up like a comma. I could see Mom had dark circles under her eyes from not sleeping. How come she hardly ever used concealer in real life? It was the cheapest, easiest effect you could buy.

"You're back so soon?" I asked.

"Scheduling mess-up. Too many nurses on the floor. So I let Krystal have my hours."

"You mean you just gave her your shift? Why?"

"Because she's my friend, and she'd already hired a babysitter for Tucker. What are you doing?"

"Watching makeup videos. I finished my homework an hour ago, so."

She frowned as she reached over to stroke Cyrus. "Wren, you watch way too much. And it feels like you're by yourself too often."

Was she really saying this? "But *you* watch TV all the time!"

"We're not discussing me. And besides, it's how I relax after work." Her forehead wrinkled. "I thought you promised to make some friends—"

"Yes, and I have! Poppy comes over here all the time!"

"Not *all* the time; you said she has soccer, right? And is this girl your *only* friend? Because you know middle school friends can change on a dime. Remember what happened with Annika?"

I swallowed hard. Why did she need to remind me about that?

"Well, I'm also friends with a kid named Kai," I lied.

It was a strange thing to say, but I was feeling desperate. What did Mom want from me, anyway? I was fine with just Poppy, so why wasn't that enough for her? It wasn't like Mom was BFFs with a million other nurses at her hospital, only the one named Krystal.

Besides—and I knew it sounded funny to say this, even to myself—but with Cat FX, I didn't feel lonely. She was sort of a friend by now. Not in a creepy-online-predator sort of way; I'd never try to contact her or anything. I just mean she was someone who shared my *actual interest*. And made me feel like I wasn't the only person on the planet who cared about liquid latex and purple lip liner.

"Wren, look," Mom said, sighing. "I just don't want you to get too isolated. It's part of why we moved here: for you to have a better social life. And I really don't think it's healthy to spend so much time alone, on your computer. I know you like those makeup videos, and that's fine, but sometimes I think you watch them to avoid being with people." She chewed her lower lip. "So here's the deal."

There's a deal? My stomach flipped like a caught fish.

"Unless you start socializing more, joining some activities at school or whatever, there'll be no more computer time," Mom said.

"Wait, *what*?" I was so loud, Cyrus jumped off the bed and scooted down the hallway. "Mom, you can't do that!"

Her eyes opened wide. "I can't? Why can't I?"

"Because I need my laptop to do homework!"

"Yes, I know. Krystal says I can switch off your internet, though. There are these parental locks you can use—"

"But sometimes I need the internet *for* homework. Like for social studies! And science!"

"Well, that'll be a problem, then."

I couldn't believe what Mom was saying. "Why are you talking about me with Krystal? She doesn't even know me!"

"Krystal is someone I respect a lot. And she's been through some inappropriate computer use with Tyndall."

"Okay, but that has nothing to do with me! Anyway, watching makeup videos isn't *inappropriate*!"

Mom stood, like she was ending the conversation. "Wren, I didn't come in here to fight with you."

"Why did you come in here, then?"

"Actually, to apologize for yelling at you before work. I was just grouchy from my headache. But it wasn't fair to take it out on you."

"Yeah, it wasn't," I said. "And my bathroom isn't messy, anyway. Or stinky."

"I know. I'm sorry I said all that." Mom lingered by my door. "But, Wren? I'm serious about that computer. If I don't see you making some efforts to socialize, I'll have to take it away. And that's not what either of us wants, so please don't make me do that, okay?"

My throat was so tight and achy I couldn't even answer.

"And don't go complaining about me to your father," she called over her shoulder as she left my room. "This has nothing to do with him. Or Vanessa."

Elphaba

hat's how I decided to do makeup for *Wicked*. Although "decided" wasn't exactly the right word, because it wasn't like I had a choice. I hadn't changed my mind about doing makeup on all those kids. But I couldn't imagine how else to suddenly "socialize." And the thought of not having my computer, not getting to see the latest Cat FX videos, was too awful to even consider.

So I just gave up. Gave in.

Plus, there was another thing on my mind besides the computer. Ever since Poppy had first brought up doing makeup for the show, she'd been waiting for my answer. At first I kept telling her I was "still thinking about it," and she seemed okay with that. But over the last few days I'd been having the feeling that she was getting impatient, maybe pulling away a little. And that was definitely making me nervous.

So the morning after that fight with Mom, I asked Poppy if she'd come with me to talk to the show director, Ms. Belfonte. "About doing makeup," I said, so Poppy wouldn't think I suddenly wanted a singing-dancing-acting part.

Poppy threw her arms around me as if I'd just scored the winning soccer goal. "Seriously, Wren? You *will*?"

I nodded. No point telling her about Mom's blackmail.

She grabbed my arm and dragged me over to our homeroom teacher, Mr. Owen. "Wren and I need to see a teacher," she informed him. "It's extremely important."

Mr. Owen was a nervous first-year teacher who seemed terrified of Poppy.

"Sure, go ahead," he said, not even asking who the teacher was.

Ms. Belfonte was arranging chairs in the chorus room. She smiled as we entered.

"This is Wren, the special-effects makeup genius I was telling you about," Poppy announced.

Ugh. No pressure.

"I'm actually just a beginner," I said quickly. "But Poppy said you might need some help with the show . . . ?"

"Yes, I certainly do." Ms. Belfonte had olive skin, a black bob, and slightly uneven bangs. She was wearing a deep red lipstick color I thought I recognized: Futuristic by Priyanka, or something close. "And you've done stage makeup before?" she asked as she studied my face.

"Oh, definitely," Poppy said, beaming.

"*No.*" I cleared my throat. "I mean, I've practiced a little on Poppy. And on my mom. And also on . . . friends where I used to live. But never for a show—"

"You should see her work, though," Poppy cut in. "Wren does all these incredible fantasy creatures. Aliens and monsters and mermaids. Plus skin conditions!"

I threw Poppy a look. "Only Poison Ivy. Although basically that was just a bunch of blisters."

"Well, it all sounds awesome." Ms. Belfonte smiled neutrally, like a nurse taking your temperature. "But doing the makeup for this musical is a very big job. We'll have plenty of parents helping out with the chorus. Although we do need someone with real expertise for Elphaba, the Wicked Witch, and maybe one or two others. Are you familiar with the show?"

"Just in general." I hoped I wasn't blushing. "I've seen Elphaba on tons of makeup videos, so."

"Wren watches makeup videos *constantly*," Poppy said. "It's *all she does*, basically. She's like *obsessed*."

Poppy was making me sound bad weird. And kind of agreeing with Mom, actually.

But Ms. Belfonte seemed interested. "I'll tell you what,

Wren. All the kids who want to be in the show need to audition. So what if I asked you to audition to be makeup artist? If you could do Elphaba makeup on someone, and take a photo, I'll be happy to have a look and consider you for the job. How does that sound?"

"Perfect," Poppy answered. "She'll get on it today!"

Ms. Belfonte smiled and started moving chairs again.

Outside the chorus room, I sucked in some oxygen. "Whoa. I have to do Elphaba *this afternoon*? That's kind of short notice."

Poppy flicked her hand. "Nah. You'll be fine. Ms. Belfonte just wants a rough draft, anyway."

I did a panicky mental inventory of the two shoeboxes: I still had some Landscape Green pigment I'd asked Mom to buy me a few weeks ago, and plenty of black eyeliner, but not the right kind of eyebrow pencil, probably. Or the right shade of purple eye shadow. According to Cat FX, when you were doing green characters—Gamora, Shrek, Hulk, the Grinch, Green Lantern—purple eye shadow was just as important as green pigment; it was the only color (besides black) that really showed up, so you needed it for contouring, especially around the eyes. But it couldn't be any old purple. Cat FX recommended Purple Haze by some company I'd never even heard of.

Probably my best purple eye shadow was the one in my

Vanessa box—Deepest Mauve by Gawjuss Makeup. But would that shade pop against the green? I wasn't sure.

"You'll come over after school today, right?" I begged Poppy.

"Today?" Poppy shook her head. "Sorry. Soccer practice, remember?"

"Wait, you *can't*?" I stared at Poppy. "Why'd you tell Ms. Belfonte I'd do it today, then?"

"Wren, I'm not the only kid in the seventh grade," she said. Not meanly. Just stating a fact. "Why don't you ask someone else to model for you?"

"Like who?" I asked, shouting over the bell for first period.

"I don't know. How about Avery? She's definitely getting Elphaba, so—"

"Avery?" I thought of her flickering-light-bulb smile, the judgy way she looked at me. If she looked at me at all. "Uh, Poppy. Wait, no—"

But she'd already run down the hall to catch Avery and Minna at the door of math class. I didn't know what else to do, so I followed.

Poppy was waving her arms as she explained about my "audition."

"And since you're *so* getting Elphaba," she was telling Avery, "Wren should practice the makeup on you, okay?"

Avery's eyes met mine for a millisecond.

"I don't know, maybe," she said.

A Little Peek

My heart pinballed the rest of the school day.

I don't know, maybe.

What did that mean? I told myself I was still psyched out by the Annika business, that I shouldn't assume it meant Avery hated me.

Plus, it really sounded like Poppy agreed with Mom—I needed to socialize more. Socialize with someone besides just Poppy, I mean. And if that was what Poppy thought, she might get annoyed with me if I didn't. If I didn't even *try*.

I decided to wait outside school at dismissal. I'd give Avery ten minutes. If she didn't show up, I'd just leave.

I watched as the seventh grade got on school buses, or started walking home with their friends. Everyone in a group of two or three or four other kids—except for

Kai, who was reading his phone as he left the building.

After four minutes, I started walking.

When I got home, first I checked the mail. No packages from Vanessa. Disappointing, but also a relief, really. Fewer things I'd need to hide.

Then I opened the door. A small, square-shaped woman in sky-blue scrubs was standing in the kitchen washing dishes.

I was so startled, I yelped.

She turned off the faucet and smiled at me. "You're Wren?" she said, extending her hand for me to shake. Like I was a grown-up. "Hi. I'm your mom's friend Krystal. We work together at the hospital."

"You're . . . her nurse friend?"

Krystal laughed. She had very short, dyed-blond hair that framed her pinkish face—strong cheekbones and a narrow chin. Wide eyes and a smooth brow. A good face for makeup.

"Yeah, we work together in the ER," she said. "But your mom wasn't feeling well, so our supervisor sent her home. And I came with her to make sure she's okay."

"Is she? Okay?"

"Of course, honey. It's just a stomach bug, so she needs to rest and drink plenty of liquids—water or plain tea."

Krystal dried her hands on a paper towel. "You know, hospitals are the germiest places on earth, and nurses are the first to catch whatever's going around."

"That's what Mom says."

"Yes, well. You should listen to what she tells you."

"Oh, I do," I said.

"Good." The way Krystal fixed me with her gray-blue eyes, I could tell she was the sort of nurse who patients never disobeyed. "Because with everything on her mind, I mean with your dad and all, she can't be worrying about you, too."

I chewed my lip. Who was this stranger telling me how to act with my own mom? And talking about my dad like she even knew him?

I wished I could stick up for myself, even though she was a grown-up.

Krystal walked over to the fridge. "Okay if I take a little peek?"

I nodded, because what else could I say?

She opened the refrigerator door. We didn't have a ton of food—Mom hadn't shopped in a few days—but there was some leftover veggie lasagna in a casserole dish. Plus milk, eggs, cheddar cheese, orange juice, apples. And three bagels in a plastic bag on the counter, next to a jar of extra-crunchy Skippy.

I could tell Krystal was satisfied that even if Mom couldn't cook tonight, I wouldn't starve.

Still, before she left, she insisted on giving me her telephone number "just in case."

I was so relieved that she was leaving that I didn't ask in case of what.

Bedroom Door

As soon as Krystal left, I took Lulu outside to pee, then went upstairs to Mom's room. Her door was shut.

I opened it a crack. She was in bed, not asleep. Reading her phone. Looking tired.

"You okay?" I called softly.

She groaned. "Yeah. I could have stayed at work—"

"Krystal said you caught a stomach bug."

"Maybe. There's all this stuff going around the ER." She put down her phone and looked at me with dead-serious eyes. "Wren, you know, if my door is shut, you shouldn't just *open* it."

I swallowed. *Is she going to start scolding me again?* "Sorry, Mom. I just wanted to see if you needed something—"

"Thanks, but I really *don't*." Her voice was harsh. Even she heard it, I thought, because she cleared her throat and said more normally, "So anyway, how was school?"

"Okay. I joined the musical. They're doing *Wicked*, and I asked if I could do makeup."

Mom's eyes got big. "You *did*? Oh Wren, that's great news!"

"But first I need to audition." I explained how Ms. Belfonte wanted to see my wicked-witch makeup. By tomorrow. And I didn't see how that was even possible.

"Do it on me," Mom said. "I always wanted to play Elphaba."

"On you? But, Mom, you're sick!"

"I'm already feeling better, sweetheart. Just give me an hour, and I'll be fine."

"How do you know that?"

"Because I'm a nurse, in case you've forgotten! Anyhow, if I'm slightly green, we're already halfway to Elphaba, right?" She smiled a little. "But right now I just need to rest. So shut the door, okay?"

"Sure," I said as I left the room. And then I thought this: *If Mom's door is shut, that means I have privacy too.*

I went into my room and reached under the bed for the other shoebox—Vanessa's, not Mom's. If I used Vanessa's Deepest Mauve for contouring, would Mom even notice? Probably not—she once told me she barely saw the difference between blush shades like Camellia and Medium Rose.

When Mom didn't come downstairs for supper, I nuked some lasagna. *Maybe she isn't better after all,* I thought.

Which means I'll have to practice Elphaba on myself.

Okay, then.

But just as I finished washing the dishes, Mom was in the kitchen in her lavender fleece bathrobe.

"Ready for my close-up now, dahling," she said, sucking in her cheeks in that joke-Hollywood way. She didn't even look tired anymore, which was kind of surprising, considering how awful she'd looked just a couple of hours ago.

"You want some supper, dahling?" I asked. "There's more lasagna—"

"Later, dahling," she said, winking. "Beauty first."

I ran upstairs to get the Mom shoebox.

And, just like I'd guessed, Mom didn't realize the eye shadow was Vanessa's. The whole time I was applying the Deepest Mauve over green pigment, Mom chatted about Krystal and her cute little son Tucker. I didn't listen; I was concentrating hard on Elphaba. Feeling jittery about using Vanessa's makeup, but also relieved that Mom seemed better. She even made witch faces when I took photos to show Ms. Belfonte.

"Thanks for doing this," I told her. "Really."

Mom blew me a Hollywood kiss as she scrolled through the photos. "Well, dahling, I can see I'm defying gravity," she said. "And you know what, Wren-with the-silent-*W*? So are you."

My heart glowed, and I forgave her for everything.

Real Eye

The next day at the start of lunch period, I showed Ms. Belfonte the Elphaba photos.

"Wren, this is just *amazing*," she said.

"I'm only doing what they say in makeup videos," I said. "It's not that hard. Just like following a recipe."

"Well, I follow recipes all the time, and I still can't roast a chicken." She grinned. "Can I see any other photos of your work?"

Ulp. I hadn't expected that.

I showed her me as Nebula and Gamora, Mom as Bride of Frankenstein, and Mom as Creepy Broken Doll. Then Poppy as a mermaid. Poppy with Poison Ivy Rash. Poppy with Frostbite. Even Poppy with Too Much Makeup.

"Although that one's kind of a mess," I added.

Ms. Belfonte looked at each photo for a too-long minute, then gave me back my phone. *"Well.* I have to say I'm *extremely impressed* with these, Wren. You have a real eye! And yes, of course I'd be delighted to have you do Elphaba for the show."

Her praise made me feel like Wren, braver and bigger. "Ms. Belfonte? Can I ask a question—what about supplies?"

"Oh, no worries. We have a decent collection of stage makeup. Nothing too fancy—"

"Well, but for Elphaba there's some stuff I need *specifically.* I mean, if you want her to look like people expect."

"Oh. Of course." Ms. Belfonte nodded. "Why don't you make a list."

I guess I looked too excited, because right away she added, "But let's keep it short, okay? Just the necessities. I'm afraid we're on a pretty tight budget with this production."

"Just the necessities," I repeated, already making the list.

In the lunchroom Poppy was sitting with Avery, Minna, Camila, Emmett, and a few other kids I never talked to, joking and laughing. Right away Poppy waved me over.

"Well? What happened with Ms. Belfonte?" she demanded.

"She liked the photo," I admitted.

"And? And?"

I shrugged. "She said I could do the makeup for the show."

Poppy screamed and threw her arms around me.

"Hey, Wren, that's awesome," Emmett said. He reached across the table to fist-bump.

"Yeah, congratulations," Camila said, smiling.

"Cool," Minna murmured, and even Avery nodded.

I had a funny feeling right then, like I was floating above the table, looking down at myself. And hearing my own voice saying, *See, Wren? This is how it looks when you finally fit in.*

The Lock

In our mailbox that afternoon was a small brown padded envelope from Effex Makeup, Ltd. My heart racing, I stuffed it into my backpack. Then I went inside.

"Mom? You home?" I called as I put the rest of today's mail—a couple of bills, a catalog from some nurses' uniform company—on the kitchen counter.

Mom didn't answer. She hadn't left a note on the counter, the way she always did if she'd gone to work. So maybe she was upstairs.

I raced up the steps, too excited to take Lulu out to pee first.

"Mom? Mom?" I yelled. "Guess what!"

Her door was shut.

Blanking on everything that had happened yesterday—how she'd scolded me for opening her door when she was in bed, the dead-serious look in her eyes when I did—I reached for the doorknob. But her door stayed shut tight. I couldn't get it to budge, not even a little.

Also, the knob felt different in my hand. I couldn't tell how, exactly, but it did.

I crouched to look: The knob had a lock. Like for a small key.

I'd never noticed it before. Was it new? It had to be.

Why did Mom need a lock for her door?

Suddenly I heard her voice coming from her bedroom, loud and muffled at the same time. From all the pauses I could tell she was on the phone.

"Yes, I know we agreed on holidays! That's not why I'm upset, okay? . . . Because you're just being really selfish. . . . Okay, but if Wren's in New York for Thanksgiving, I'll be here all by myself. You do realize that, Peter, right?"

My insides froze.

I backed away from the door and went downstairs to take care of Lulu. Then back upstairs to my bedroom.

I unzipped my backpack to get the small brown envelope, which I stuffed, unopened, into the Vanessa shoebox.

Mom's voice cut through the small house like a big, dull knife.

From my desk I couldn't make out all the words, but I knew this much: My parents were fighting again. About me. About Thanksgiving, which was two weeks away.

When I'd visited the babies for Halloween, Dad and Vanessa had mentioned my returning for the holiday weekend; it wasn't a specific plan or anything, just like, *Hey, we should think about your next visit! Because it's hard to get plane tickets around Thanksgiving.*

And when I got home from New York, I didn't tell Mom what they said, because I could see she was having a hard time about the babies. And anyhow, I told myself, all the parent-schedule stuff wasn't my job to figure out.

"All you ever care about is yourself. And Vanessa—"

Did Mom think I wouldn't hear her shouting? Maybe she didn't realize I was home.

I turned on my laptop. *Just tune her out,* I told myself. *Research purple eye shadows for Ms. Belfonte's list. Something not expensive.*

But this was hard, because there were like sixty zillion different shades of purple: Royal Purple, Purple Mountain Majesty, Vivid Orchid, Cyber Grape, Petunia, Phlox—

"You know what, Peter? We're not one big happy family; we're *two separate ones* now, okay? And Wren is the only family I have, so when it's a holiday—"

Very Berry, Neon Purple, Palest Lavender, Aubergine, Purple Prose, Shy Violet.

Thistle, Purple Rain, Lilac . . .

o O o

About an hour later, Mom was standing in my doorway.

"Hey," she said, smiling a little too brightly.

"Hi, Mom," I said.

"Well? How was school?"

"It was okay."

"Just okay?" She cocked her head, still smiling. "What happened with those Elphaba photos?"

I shrugged. "Ms. Belfonte liked them. She said I could do makeup for the show. So I'm, you know. Socializing. Like you said."

"Wren, that's wonderful!" She ran over to hug me. "I'm so proud of you, honeybee! I knew that teacher would be impressed if she could just see your work! You should never be shy about showing anyone what you can do!"

Her hug felt good, but for some reason I couldn't wait for it to be over.

When she finally pulled away, I said, "Mom? I heard you on the phone before. If you really don't want me to visit Dad for Thanksgiving—"

"No, no, sweetheart, it's okay! Dad and I worked it all out. I just don't like surprises. Or feeling like plans are being made behind my back."

My face burned. "But I didn't! I'd *never* go behind your back—"

"Oh, I didn't mean *you*; I meant your father. Anyway, everything's fine now. Of course you'll go to Brooklyn for the holiday. They're doing a big fancy meal. Grandma Ellen will be there, and you haven't seen her since the wedding."

Grandma Ellen was Dad's mom. Mom had been raised by her own grandma, a strict woman she called Gigi, who died when I was a baby. I knew how much Mom liked Grandma Ellen; she probably missed her, and that made me sad. Why did a divorce mean you lost your relatives? Family was supposed to be forever.

Mom started walking to the door.

I hadn't planned to say anything, but before she could leave, it just came out. "Hey, can I ask a question? Did you put a lock on your door?"

She stopped. Then she turned around and smiled her too-bright smile again. "Yes, actually, I did. I had a locksmith stop by while you were at school today."

"How come?"

"Just to keep the cat off my bed," she replied. Then she turned and went downstairs to the kitchen.

Audition

After that, Mom locked her door every night when she went to bed, and kept it locked all day while she was at work. She didn't say anything else about it, and neither did I, mostly because I'd be leaving soon for Thanksgiving in Brooklyn and didn't want to start another fight.

The Monday before Thanksgiving weekend, Ms. Belfonte had auditions for *Wicked*. The drama kids were talking about it all the time—what part they wanted, the song they'd choose for the tryout, what they'd wear. None of these conversations had anything to do with me. But I didn't feel left out, because Poppy made sure I was always included. Once she even announced to everyone at lunch that I was "one of the most important parts of the whole production."

So of course, when it was time for Poppy to audition, I offered to come to cheer her on.

"Would you, Wren?" she said. "I really want you to be there! Except"—she turned hot pink and started giggling—"I'll be super self-conscious if you watch."

"You want me to be there, but not *be* there?" I teased.

"Yes, exactly! If that's okay! What I mean is, could you just stay outside the auditorium and wait for me? But not be inside when I'm actually singing?"

"Sure," I said. "Although I'm sure you'll do great."

"Haha, really? That's because you've never heard me sing!"

She was right; I hadn't. But I thought it was strange to see her this nervous about performing. Probably she was exaggerating how bad she was, the way some kids swore they'd fail a test before they took it, or claimed they were ugly just so you'd tell them they weren't.

The truth was, I had a hard time thinking of Poppy as bad at anything. The more I knew her, the more I thought she was everything I wished I was: Happy all the time. Nice to everybody. Outgoing and chatty. Athletic.

Sometimes the more you knew someone, the less amazing they seemed. But with Poppy, it was the opposite—the more I knew her, the more I wanted to be her friend. So even though Lulu was waiting for me at home, I sat on the floor outside the auditorium doors, doing math homework, for thirty-five minutes.

When the doors finally flew open, though, it wasn't Poppy who came out. It was Kai, one of the kids (according to Poppy) too weird to be doing the show. Although, for some reason, he'd been inside the auditorium the whole time while kids auditioned.

"Hello, Wren," he said politely while I stared at him. "Why are you sitting here?"

"Just waiting for someone."

"Who? Poppy?"

"Yep." I stood up. He'd noticed that Poppy and I were friends? I hadn't realized he paid attention to anything besides his phone.

Now that we were facing each other, about a foot apart, I could see directly into Kai's face. And I'd been right—he did have one blue eye and one brown eye! I'd never seen a person like that before, not in real life. Did any of Cat FX's characters have two different eye colors too? I couldn't think of one offhand, but that didn't mean there weren't any.

Maybe Kai realized I was staring, because he frowned and looked away. "Well, she just finished in there, so she'll be out soon." He paused, like he wasn't sure if he should keep talking.

Then he blurted: "Although she's pretty much the worst singer I ever heard. No offense."

I felt my cheeks burning. "Why do you think I'd be offended?"

"I don't know. Because she's your friend?"

"Right, Poppy *is* my friend. And neither of us cares about your opinion. In case you were wondering."

His face crumpled. "Sorry, Wren," he mumbled, and walked away fast.

For a second I felt bad about hurting his feelings. But when Poppy came out a few minutes later, she seemed her usual chatty self, as if the audition had gone perfectly fine. So I decided Kai didn't know what he was talking about. And I didn't tell Poppy about his rude comment, or how I'd defended her and her singing.

Thanksgiving

Three days later, I was in New York for Thanksgiving, eating turkey and stuffing and Vanessa's homemade pumpkin pie. To be honest, I didn't like pumpkin pie—the filling slipped down my throat in an upsetting way—but Dad made such a fuss about Vanessa's baking, how it wasn't easy for her, since she was also nursing two screaming babies. So I had a big slice and told her it was delicious.

"Vanessa is the *best*," Dad gushed. "The *best*."

"Oh, stop it, Peter," Vanessa said, laughing.

They kissed at the table, which was definitely embarrassing. But also happy. But also awful, because it made me think of Mom home all by herself, probably snoozing on the sofa, or locked in her bedroom, reading her phone or watching/not-watching TV.

And later, when Grandma Ellen asked me how "Kelly"

was doing, for a second I didn't know how to answer.

"Mom is fine," I told her. Thinking: *Maybe you call her Kelly, but I still call her Mom.*

"Well, I'm very glad to hear that," Grandma Ellen replied. "You know, I've never wished her anything but the best."

"All right, Mom," Dad said, ending the conversation with his eyes.

"Sorry we won't be able to hit Sephora while you're here," Vanessa told me later as we loaded the dishwasher. "I thought we might be able to go, but with these two naughty munchkins, I'm not sure that's the best idea." She kissed Paxton's cheek and rubbed Ayla's belly, and they both wiggled and gurgled in their baby seats while we cleaned.

"That's okay," I said quickly. "Anyhow, I've been meaning to thank you for all the stuff you've been sending. You really don't have to—"

"Oh, but it's my pleasure, Wren! We artists need to stick together."

I smiled and nodded, happy that she considered the two of us "artists." Although a teeny bit uncomfortable, too, because of course Vanessa was a terrible painter. Since my last visit, she'd started a bunch of paintings she called "waterscapes": snot-colored rivers, oceans with soapy-looking whitecaps, ponds with heart-shaped algae. In all these pictures, the sky was a bright, cheery blue, even if the water was murky. This blue really bothered me, and sometimes I worried she'd want to hang one of these "waterscapes" in my room. But since she never finished them, it wasn't actually a problem.

Anyway, however I felt about Vanessa's work, I liked how much she cared about art supplies, always choosing the best paints and brushes. And even though I felt guilty that she kept buying me expensive makeup—*behind Mom's back*—I was glad that we had this connection.

So when she asked if I needed any new makeup products, I thought about all the stuff I needed for *Wicked*, and how Ms. Belfonte said we were on a tight budget.

"Another Deepest Mauve would be great," I admitted. "Also, if you can, some more Landscape Green pigment, some Magenta Magic blush, and a bottle of setting spray. Not for me, for the show," I added.

"Anything your dad and I can do to help," Vanessa said, reaching out to give me one of her hugs. "Anything you need from us, ever."

"Thank you," I said. And I meant it.

But even with all of Vanessa's niceness and generosity, I couldn't stop thinking how she and Dad and the babies were now an "us." And I wasn't *in* Dad's new family, not really.

o O o

On Saturday, just before I was about to leave, Dad came into my room, sat on the futon (which still had the babyish kite quilt), and put his arm around my shoulders. "Rennie, I'm really happy to see how close you're getting with Vanessa. I knew you two would hit it off."

"She's really great," I said. "But you shouldn't call me Rennie anymore. Remember, Dad? I'm Wren now."

"Sorry! *Wren.* I'll try to get it right." He scratched his head. "So. I wanted a chance to catch up a little before you left. How's it going in the new school? Nice teachers?"

"They're okay."

"And the other kids?"

"I'm making friends, Dad. Don't worry."

"Oh, I'm not *worried*, jellybean. Because *I* know how cool you are." He grinned. "And how's Mom?"

Dad says "Mom," which is better than "Kelly."

Mom says "your father."

"Fine," I said.

My heart picked up speed. *Should I mention the lock on her door?* There was nothing to say about it, really. Just that it was a little . . . weird. "Why are you asking?"

"*Why?*" Dad squinted at me. "I need a special reason?"

"No. But you guys are divorced now, so." I shrugged.

Dad paused a few seconds. Then he said, "You know, sweetheart, I still care about Mom very much. A divorce doesn't erase what we shared as a family."

It was good to hear Dad say that. But still, if he wanted to know how Mom was doing, couldn't he just ask her himself? It wasn't like they never talked on the phone. Why was he asking *me*?

Maybe he wanted me to tattle on her. Tell him about the lock, or just complain about the socializing-at-school stuff. But if I told him how she'd blackmailed me about computer time, it would probably get back to her, and then she'd be furious I'd been complaining about her to Dad. And anyhow, lately I'd been thinking Mom had been right to make me do the play. I mean, it was definitely scary, and not something I could even think about without stomach jitters, but the truth was it was helping me to fit in better.

Just like Mom had been right about moving to Donwood. She knew me more than I wanted to admit sometimes.

"Mom's working hard," I said. "Doing a lot of overtime. She's made friends with this other nurse named Krystal." Dad was smiling, but I could see in his eyes that he didn't want to hear about Krystal.

"Hand sandwich," he said, so I let him take my hand. "Okay, jellybean, I'm happy everything's good for you both.

I wish we got to see you more often, but I want you to know you can always call me. Day or night."

Now my face was hot. "About what?" I said. "What would I call you about?"

"Anything," Dad replied, still smiling, still sandwiching my hand. "Anything at all."

Phish Food

Mom seemed cheerful when she picked me up at the airport on Saturday night. On the car ride home she let me talk about Ayla and Paxton a little before changing the subject. She even smiled as I described Vanessa's slippery pumpkin pie.

When we pulled into our driveway, she turned off the car but didn't get out. "So," she said. "I have a question I need to ask. Did they say anything about me?"

"What do you mean?" I asked.

"I mean your father and Vanessa. Were they talking about me? To you?"

"No, of course not!" My brain scrambled. Dad had *asked* about Mom—*asking* wasn't the same as *talking about*, was it? And I'd answered without saying anything private. At least I was pretty sure I had.

"Listen, sweetheart." Mom sighed. "I'm very sorry you have to do all this back-and-forth between two houses. I'm sorry you need to deal with a divorce. But you have two separate families now. And as long as you'll be visiting Brooklyn so much, I need you to promise me one thing: you'll never talk about me behind my back."

My mouth dropped open. "Mom, why would I—"

"It's not fair for you to be in the middle, I know. And frankly, this divorce is hard enough on *me* without feeling like I'm being gossiped about, or analyzed, or pitied. Especially by your father and his beautiful young new wife."

But how did Mom even know how Vanessa looked? They hadn't met. Maybe she'd seen a photo online.

I considered explaining that only Dad ever asked about her; Vanessa never even said her name. But I wasn't sure that would make it better.

"Vanessa isn't like that," I said lamely. "She's actually a very nice person. She likes to paint."

Mom's forehead wrinkled. "Let's not discuss her. Just promise me, Wren. It's all I need to hear from you, okay?"

I promised.

"Thank you," she said, and kissed my cheek.

Then she got out of the car, went to her bedroom, and locked the door.

∘ O ∘

When Mom came out of her room about an hour later, she stood outside my room and called softly, "Wren, honey? You awake? Want to watch a movie? I bought us Phish Food."

Our favorite ice cream. She didn't buy it often, and whenever she did, the two of us split the pint in one sitting.

I can't say why, but I didn't answer. My lights were off, and I'd brought my laptop into bed, so I just pretended to be asleep.

I heard her go downstairs to the kitchen, open the freezer, and turn on the TV in the living room.

Then I watched twelve Cat FX videos in a row.

Hey, guys, another secret message for you: You can be anyone or anything you choose. A happy unicorn. A creepy cyborg. A beautiful, mysterious mermaid. The only limit is your imagination.

Wicked

CONGRATULATIONS, CAST OF WICKED!

We were so impressed with all who auditioned for this year's spring musical, and assigning parts was a really difficult decision! But we're confident that every student will find some important way to be involved—onstage and backstage!

Here's the FINAL CAST LIST:
Boq: Elias Rothberg, Grade 8
Dr. Dillamond: Mateo Ruiz, Grade 7
Elphaba: Avery Jamison, Grade 7
Fiyero: Emmett Brooker, Grade 7
Glinda: Gracie Ng, Grade 8

Hey, where was Poppy on this list?

Madame Morrible: Minna Choudhry, Grade 7
Nessarose: Camila Bak, Grade 7
The Wizard: Jonas Riordan, Grade 8
Dr. Nikidik: Poppy Fairbanks, Grade 7

My heart sank. I'd never even heard of Dr. Nikidik, which probably meant Poppy didn't have a big role. Maybe not even a singing one.

And Avery was Elphaba, just like everyone knew she'd be.

Why did they even have auditions if all the parts were already decided? Probably they'd been decided last year, or the year before. That was how middle school was, really: You got judged one day at the very beginning, and that was it forever. Nothing you could do to change anyone's opinion.

Poor Poppy—she'll be so disappointed, I thought. *Just like Kai predicted.*

And for a reason I couldn't explain, I suddenly felt furious at Kai.

Poppy was four minutes late for homeroom that morning. When she finally showed up, she went straight over to Avery and gave her a big hug. Avery said thank you and how totally *shocked* she was and omigod it was such a hard part, really scary to sing all those songs, maybe she couldn't do it? But her eyes sparkled and her face glowed. She wasn't shocked or scared at all, I thought; she just knew you were supposed to pretend that you were.

As for Poppy: I'd looked up Dr. Nikidik on my phone. And I'd guessed right—it was a teeny part. One scene, no singing. Poppy would barely be onstage. She had to be disappointed, but she was too nice a friend not to congratulate Avery.

When the bell rang for homeroom, I walked over to Poppy. Up close, I could see her eyes and nose looked rabbity pink. Had she been crying? It was hard to imagine Poppy sad about anything.

"Hey," I said softly.

"Hey, Wren." She threw her backpack over one shoulder as we walked out into the hallway. "You saw the cast list?"

"Yeah," I said. "I did. Poppy, I'm really sorry—"

"*Don't* be, okay? I talked to Ms. Belfonte during homeroom, and she said if I want, I can *also* be a flying monkey. So I get to swoop around the stage!" Poppy did her waterfall laugh, which for the first time sounded a little forced to me. "Plus I'm in the ensemble!"

"That means the chorus?"

"Yeah. And this way I'll also have time for winter

volleyball. Anyhow, the person you should feel sorry for is Minna. Because it wasn't like I assumed I was getting anything. But she really wanted Glinda."

"But Minna got Madame Morrible, right? Is that a big part?"

Poppy frowned. "Wren, don't you know *anything* about the show?"

"A little." My face was burning. "I've mostly focused on Elphaba's makeup."

Poppy stopped in front of the math room. She was still frowning. "*Wicked* is about friendship. And love. And being brave, and thinking for yourself. You should really listen to the cast album, or watch some videos. Because you know, Wren, the whole thing's not just about *makeup*."

Her voice had a sharpness I'd never heard before.

I spent the rest of that day with a hollow feeling in my stomach, convinced that Poppy was done with our friendship—that she saw how little we had in common. How weird I was, obsessed with something no one else cared about.

And I couldn't stop hearing Mom's voice in my head: *Middle school friends can change on a dime. Remember what happened with Annika?*

Dog Robots

That night around nine my phone rang. But not Dad this time. Poppy.

"Hey, Wren," she said. "Can you talk a sec?"

I said sure, as I jumped up from my desk to shut my bedroom door. Which was crazy, really, because Mom was at the hospital.

"What's up?" I asked as casually as I could, even though my heart was speeding.

"I just wanted to apologize," Poppy said. "I was kind of nasty to you at school today. And I feel terrible about it."

"Oh, Poppy, you weren't nasty! And you were right, I should definitely learn about the show. I was being stupid—"

"No, no, you were fine. I just came down on you because I was upset about the cast list." She paused. "And I have this thing about hiding how I feel. Always acting happy, even when I'm really not."

This startled me. "Then why do you act happy?"

"Because people think that's how I am. *Who* I am."

"Okay, but *you* decide that, right? Not other people."

"I guess."

I chewed my lower lip. If I was ever going to share my secret, now was the time, obviously. "Can I tell you something, Poppy?"

"Sure."

"Okay. So." I took a breath. "My name wasn't always Wren."

"It wasn't?"

"Yeah, it used to be Renata. But I changed it."

"Seriously? How come?"

"Because it didn't feel like . . . who I am."

"Whoa." Poppy breathed loudly. "That. Is. So. Cool."

"Thanks."

"I mean it! And you're *definitely* a Wren! I can't even *imagine* you as a Renata." She laughed. "You know what? I kind of hate the name Poppy. But if I ever changed it, my mom would kill me. Was your mom mad?"

"Actually, no. She was great about it."

Then Poppy said a really shocking thing. "Oh, Wren. You're so lucky. If I could be anyone, I'd be you."

"*Me?* Are you joking? Why?"

"Because you don't care about people liking you, or being popular, or any of that stuff. You just do what you want. Not only with your name, I mean." She paused. "Also, your mom seems really great."

I nodded, even though of course Poppy couldn't see.

Mom barely mentioned me spending winter break in Brooklyn until two days before I was supposed to leave. Then all of a sudden at breakfast she asked if I had presents for Ayla and Paxton.

I licked some peanut butter off my bagel and told her not to worry.

"I'm not worried," she said. "I just don't want anyone blaming *me*."

I explained how at Thanksgiving, Dad saw some drawings I'd made—dog robots on wheels—and asked if he could frame them. As my Christmas present to the family. So I was all set.

"That sounds lovely." Mom said it like she meant it. Then she took a sip of coffee.

Right then I thought of something I should have considered a lot earlier. "Mom, what will you be doing on Christmas?"

"Me? Oh, just working." She must have read my

BARBARA DEE

expression, because she added, "Hey, being at the hospital on Christmas isn't fun, but it's even less fun for the patients, okay? And let me remind you, my dear, holiday shifts pay extra. So don't feel sorry for me! Anyhow, Krystal's doing Christmas dinner at her house, and she invited me over after work."

"Really? Wow, that's so nice of her," I said enthusiastically.

"Yes, it is." She smiled. "Krystal loves to cook, so I'm sure it'll be a big, fancy meal."

Mom was trying to sound cheerful, but it wasn't working. She didn't talk much about her grandma Gigi, but I knew that Gigi had been very strict about a lot of things, including church every Sunday. Mom wasn't religious at all, and neither was Dad, who was Jewish. So we never made much fuss about Christmas *or* Chanukah: We'd get a small "holiday bush," which Dad would plant in our garden, exchange a few low-key gifts (stuff like books, jigsaw puzzles, and mittens), and light a menorah. Oh, and Dad would make latkes. That was it for both holidays.

And now here I was, abandoning Mom, going off to have a big, happy Christmas with Vanessa's big, happy family, which included two adorable babies. Plus Grandma Ellen, and probably assorted relatives from Vanessa's side of the family. Plus (obviously) Dad. From what he'd told me, I knew they'd be doing a giant blingy tree, a million presents, and a ton of food—the opposite of how we usually celebrated.

I think Mom noticed the guilt on my face. "Hey, honey-bee, you know what I'd love?" she said brightly. "If we could do some makeup tonight. You and me."

"Really? What kind?"

"You choose. But I've been thinking about your mermaid. And it might be fun to do the whole thing. Eyebrow pearls, scales, the works."

My mind raced. "Okay, sure . . . but that color still looks wrong to me. It's not shimmery, the way it looks in the video, and it's too green. And I haven't figured out a better pigment."

"Hmm. What does your YouTube person say?"

"You mean Cat FX? She says to use Seafoam Blue by CozMeticks. And she's never wrong about anything, so." I shrugged. "I keep thinking I missed something."

"Well, *everyone* makes mistakes. Even experts like Cat FX." Mom smiled. "And maybe different colors look different on different people. You know, like how not everyone reacts the same way to medicines."

A nurse thing to say. But the thing was, she was right. Cat FX said to work with all kinds of skin tones—but she'd done the Elphaba makeup on her own white skin.

Obviously, when I applied Landscape Green to Avery's Black skin, I couldn't do it the exact same way.

This thought—that I wouldn't be able to just follow Cat FX's directions—made me nervous, so I decided not to think about it right then.

"Anyhow," Mom added, "Cat FX's mermaid isn't the *only* possible version. Just invent your own, sweetheart. You can experiment on me! Because that's what moms are for, right?"

I got up from the table to hug her.

"Ugh, go wash your hands, Wren," she scolded, laughing. "You got me all sticky from that peanut butter."

Envelope

Christmas in Brooklyn was fun and noisy and messy. Vanessa had invited her brother and his family, plus two of her cousins and their five little kids—so the fancy brownstone was crammed with people who wore ugly-on-purpose sweaters with Rudolph the Red-Nosed Reindeer designs (the grown-ups), or ran around the house chasing one another and screaming the SpongeBob song (the five little kids).

Of course, there was a real tree—not a little "holiday bush"—which everyone decorated with silver snowflakes and angels that someone's great-aunt had crocheted a million years ago. Vanessa cooked a ham and a spicy fishy soup, Ayla and Paxton gurgled and spat up all over their bouncy seats, and Dad made his latkes, although only Vanessa, Grandma Ellen, and I ate any.

A big-family holiday, the kind I'd always imagined. But to be honest, I couldn't help feeling like I was watching it through a rain-streaked window, or maybe on YouTube.

The night before I was flying back home, Dad came upstairs to my room. He sat next to me on the futon, which sagged a little from the two of us.

"Rennie—*Wren*," he said, throwing his arm across my shoulders. "I feel like I've hardly had any time with you, and now you're leaving again." He made puppy eyes and did a pretend pout that made me laugh.

"Yeah, but I had fun," I said.

"I'm glad, jellybean. You know, Vanessa and I both love it when you visit. And of course Ayla and Paxton love it too." Suddenly he reached into his pocket for an envelope. "Part of your Chanuk-mas gift," he said, smiling at the word he and Mom always used for our family's not-quite-this-not-quite-that version of the holiday.

I opened the envelope. Two hundred dollars! He and Vanessa had already given me a book about special-effects makeup, a small leather journal, and a gorgeous makeup case covered in silk with a butterfly design. Also a bunch of socks with random sayings like SPOILER ALERT: THE ENDING SUCKS and EASILY DISTRACTED BY SHINY OBJECTS.

"Thank you, Dad," I said. But I couldn't help thinking about the holidays we used to have, how we never did big presents. All this money in an envelope was an amazing gift, but a little strange. And a little sad, too, somehow. "You really didn't have to—"

"Well, you're not a baby anymore, Rennie—I mean Wren. Vanessa loves buying you things, but we thought that if there's special stuff you want, that makeup you like or anything else, it'll feel good to buy it for yourself." Dad squeezed my shoulders. "Just be sure to keep those bills somewhere safe," he added.

Safe from what? I thought but didn't say.

When Mom picked me up at O'Hare Airport, she was wearing scrubs that seemed a size too big. Like maybe she'd shrunk a little since I'd left for New York.

Right away I felt the energy whoosh out of me. All this back-and-forth to New York seemed sort of pointless suddenly. Vanessa's big, loud family was nice, but they weren't *my* family. Even the Dad-Vanessa-Ayla-Paxton family seemed like a dream I had sometimes, the kind of dream where you're just the narrator. I wasn't *in* that family, not really. My real life was here with Mom, who needed me.

"How was it?" she asked as she threw her arms around me. "Did they have a big tree?"

"You really want to know?" I asked.

"Truthfully? Nope." She grinned as we stepped on the escalator to the parking lot.

I couldn't help smiling back. "Okay, so how was Krystal's?"

Her face went blank. "What do you mean?"

"I mean for Christmas. She had a big fancy dinner . . . ?"

"Oh, right. Yeah, it was great," Mom said, then frowned at something on her phone.

When we got home about an hour later, I nuzzled Lulu and held Cyrus in my lap while Mom made me a cheddar omelet and two slices of toast smothered in butter. Nothing for herself, though; she said she'd eaten before driving to the airport.

She watched while I finished the omelet, her chin resting on her fists. Like it was fascinating to watch me eat. Like I was a character in a Cat FX video.

"God, I missed you *so much*, Wren," she said. "I *hate* being here without you! Because I really love you, you know?" Then she laughed like, *Aren't I silly?*

"I love you too, Mom," I said. "And by the way, this omelet is delicious."

"Specialty of the house, dahling." Mom laughed as she got up to give me another hug. I breathed in her smell: Dove soap, plus something I couldn't identify. Maybe it was a waiting-at-the-airport smell. Or a scent she'd picked up somewhere else.

Almost like she could read my mind, she announced she needed to take a shower. I followed her upstairs to dump my duffel bag on my bed, listening as she went into her bedroom and closed the door.

And of course I heard it: *CLICK.*

I had this strange thought right then: *The whole time I was in Brooklyn, did she lock her bedroom door?*

Well, sure she did, I told myself. *To keep Cyrus off her bed.*

If that's really why she locks it. To keep Cyrus off her bed.

I unzipped my duffel bag and took out the butterfly-patterned makeup case. Carefully, organizing everything in neat rows, I transferred all the products from the Vanessa shoebox into the makeup case. Then I took the envelope of money out of my jeans pocket, tucked it into the far left corner of the case, closed the top, and pushed it under my bed, all the way to the wall.

Giant Eyeball

Hey, guys, Cat FX here. Hope you all had a great December! Mine was pretty cool. Although my dog Poochie got kennel cough and doggy diarrhea, which I'm guessing you do not want to hear about. But that's my exciting life story.

Anyway, on New Year's Day I had one of my best ideas yet. And now I'm going to share it as my special holiday gift. Are you ready? I now present . . . the Giant Eyeball.

Wait, you're laughing! Don't laugh! This effect is tricky and super cool! And you should trust me because I never lie to you guys. Ever.

Three days after I got back home, school started again, and that meant I could finally see Poppy. We'd texted each other a few times over the break, but basically just to show each other presents (my socks) and to complain about relatives (her cousins who wouldn't stop fighting).

Since the phone call when she'd apologized and I'd told her about my name, I hadn't been feeling as shaky about our friendship. But that phone call was more than a month ago. And of course I knew how popular she was, how busy she'd be with winter volleyball plus the show from now on. So that meant if I wanted to hang out with Poppy, I needed to say something fast.

"There's this new effect I'm desperate to do," I told her at the start of math. "It's called the Giant Eyeball. And I think I have most of the makeup for it. If you wanted to try."

"Giant *Eyeball*?" Poppy said it so loud that Avery snickered, and Kai looked up from his worksheet. "I don't know, Wren. It sounds pretty gross."

"Or not," I said quickly. "We can do something else if you'd rather."

Poppy rested her hand on my arm. "Yeah, fun. But not today. Ms. Belfonte called a cast meeting after school."

"Oh, okay. Some other time, then."

"Anyhow, Wren, there's a tech meeting today," Kai blurted.

I looked at him. "What?"

"For the show. For *Wicked*. You're doing makeup, right?"

"Yeah," I said.

"Well, then, you're on tech crew, technically." He was blushing. "We're meeting in the auditorium. Didn't you see the poster by the main office? With the tech-crew schedule?"

I shook my head.

"Hey, Kai, why don't you write it to Wren in a love letter," Avery said in a teasing sort of voice, and Poppy gave her arm a smack.

After school I went to the auditorium. My art teacher, Ms. Chen, was in front of the stage talking to Kai. Three other kids—two girls and a boy—were standing in the aisle, reading their phones. They looked like eighth graders, I thought. The boy had zits on his forehead; one of the girls had a purple streak in her brown hair.

"Hey there, Wren," Ms. Chen called out. "Welcome to tech crew!"

I looked at her, not at Kai. "I don't know if I'm supposed to be here, actually. I'm just doing makeup."

"Then you're on tech crew," Kai insisted.

I kept my eyes on Ms. Chen. "Am I?"

She smiled. "Well, tech includes everyone who's not performing. We're not worrying about makeup at this point; we're all multitasking for now. And we're very happy to have you join us."

Join them? I bit the inside of my cheek. This wasn't at all how I'd imagined working on the show. Maybe I could make up some excuse. *My plant needs watering. I just remembered a dentist appointment. I have to walk my three-legged dog.* That one was true, actually.

"But I can only stay thirty minutes," I said.

"Well, let's get started, then! Do you know everyone— Pippa, Aliyah, and Henry? They all worked on last year's musical, *Pippin*, so they can show you the ropes. And of course Kai's our tech whiz."

"I am not," Kai said.

"Don't be so modest," the purple-streaked girl said. "If you hadn't fixed that sound board during intermission—"

"Ugh, Pippa, don't remind us; it's bad luck," Henry said. He knocked on one of the wooden boards that Ms. Chen was stacking on the edge of the stage. "We're building scenery *already*?"

"Yep," Ms. Chen said. "No point wasting time. This is a complicated show with lots of scene changes. So we're going to need many extra flats."

"Flats?" I repeated. Already I was lost.

Ms. Chen explained that flats were four-by-eight-foot walls made out of wooden frames that were covered in cloth

BARBARA DEE

and then painted. Some of the flats they'd used in *Pippin* could be recycled and painted over, but we'd be building at least ten more, she said.

"But I've never built anything before," I said.

Ms. Chen winked at me. "Well, here's your chance to learn. Kai will show you."

All right, just leave, I urged myself. *Forget about the deal with Mom. Forget about "socializing"—because the whole point was to "socialize" with Poppy, and she's off rehearsing with the other actors. And anyhow, I agreed to do makeup, not bang on things with hammers. Especially not with Kai!*

A strange thought flashed in my brain right then: *What if I quit the show and don't tell Mom? She's always so busy with work, and so out of it when she gets home. How would she even know?*

"Wren? Are you paying attention?" Kai said. It surprised me that he sounded annoyed.

"Yeah," I said. "I guess."

He picked up a hammer and started banging.

Strings

The problem with Mom having a job with a crazy schedule was that I never knew where she'd be.

And this made it tricky to just quit tech crew. Because even when Mom was flopping-on-the-sofa tired, she paid attention to me like nobody else. So I figured if I stopped doing tech crew, it might not register with her at first, especially if she was working crazy hours. But after a few days, she'd definitely notice that I was around too much, in my room by myself—not socializing, like we'd agreed. And then she'd take away my computer and get mad at me again. Maybe even tell Krystal I was "giving her trouble."

I couldn't help thinking that if you had a normal family like Poppy's—Mom, Dad, brother, sister, all living together in the same place—it wasn't only that you felt connected to each other by invisible strings. It was also like you felt connected to your house: the walls, the floors, the ceilings, which all seemed solid and permanent. So even if you did something wrong, even if your parents got mad at you about something, the invisible strings wouldn't just snap, and you wouldn't float away.

Basically the opposite of how I'd been feeling lately.

I mean, of course I knew Mom and Dad loved me. But between all the back-and-forth flying to Brooklyn (where, despite Vanessa's niceness, I still didn't feel I belonged), and Mom's crazy schedule and her moods, I wasn't sure that our strings would hold, or that our ceilings were solid. If Mom got mad at me again—like for quitting tech crew and then lying to her about it—maybe I'd crash through the roof of our little townhouse, and just sort of drift away into the clouds.

Also, I was already hiding Vanessa's products, the fancy makeup case with the butterfly pattern, and the two hundred dollars Dad had given me for Chanuk-mas. So the thought of another secret from Mom made my stomach knot.

What I'm saying is that I decided to stick with tech crew. At least for now.

Hammer

"Wren, you're holding that hammer all wrong," Kai was saying.

We were back in the auditorium three days later, building flats. I wasn't enjoying it, exactly, but it felt good to smash some nails. Even if most of the time I missed.

Now Kai was crouching next to me, frowning.

I sighed. "All right, so what's wrong with my hammer holding?"

"You're choking up on it too much. You need to grab it near the end of the handle, and move your arm like this." He did a loose sort of swinging motion. "And don't bang so hard. Just try to meet the nail with the face of the hammer."

"Like this?" I did a super-slo-mo version of the hammer-swing. As a joke, but Kai didn't get it.

"No, actually," he said. "You're also holding the nail too

near the bottom, against the wood. You'll crush your fingers that way."

"I won't crush my fingers," I said.

"You will if you keep missing. Statistically speaking."

I groaned inside my head. Why did this kid keep giving opinions nobody asked him for? And pay attention *only to me*?

Well, I knew the answer to that question. Every time Kai said anything to me in math, Avery would make a kissy face at us, or say something like, "Aww, you two are so cuuute."

But I didn't want to crush my fingers. I mean, I needed them.

So I tried to grip the nail the way Kai said—and sure enough, this time when I hammered, the nail disappeared into the wood. Perfectly flat, too.

"Yesss!" I shouted.

Kai grinned. "See? It seems like it would be easy, right? But there's a special technique. Can I ask you a question?"

No. "I guess."

"What's the Giant Eyeball?"

I stopped hammering. "What?"

"You were talking to Poppy the other day. Is that like a character from something?"

"The Giant Eyeball? No, I'm pretty sure it's just made up."

"By who?"

"This makeup artist I follow online? *Special-effects* makeup. Her name is Cat FX, and she's really cool."

Kai nodded. "Yeah, I thought it was something like that. And that's why you did that picture of Nebula?"

"What picture?"

"The one I saw on your desk a few months ago. Of her cybernetic eye?"

He meant the drawing Poppy had noticed back in September, a million years ago. He still remembered it?

"Yeah," I said. "It was just a sketch, though. The makeup is incredibly complicated for certain characters, and sometimes it helps me to sort of map it out first."

"I'm the same way, actually. I always plan ahead. My therapist wants me to be more spontaneous."

Why was he telling me this? I made a sound like "Huh." Just to be polite.

Then he said, "Well, if you ever need someone to practice on. I mean, if Poppy isn't available."

I stared at his different-colored eyes. One blue, one brown.

"But only if you're doing superheroes or something," he added. He was blushing so hard it was like he'd applied too much Magenta Magic. "I mean, I'm not into *regular makeup*."

"Neither am I, actually. Just special effects."

"Cool," he said, a little too eagerly. "So, Wren . . . do you cosplay?"

I shook my head.

"Why not? It seems like something you'd do."

"I'm not anti-cosplay. I'm just more interested in the makeup. Than in pretending to be a specific character, I mean." As I said this, I thought about the mermaid, but she wasn't a comic-book or movie character that anyone else would recognize. Just my own private fantasy creature, and you couldn't cosplay that, probably.

Kai shrugged. "I think you might enjoy it, though."

"Maybe."

When he realized I was done talking, he walked over to Henry and Aliyah, who were possibly hammering the wrong way too.

An hour later, I waited for Poppy outside the auditorium. The cast and chorus were meeting in the band room so that Ms. Belfonte could teach them songs on her piano. And whenever Poppy wasn't staying late for some extra volleyball practice, the two of us walked home together.

Really, it was the best part of my day.

But today she showed up with Avery and Minna. They were all laughing about Emmett—how he'd been clowning around during rehearsal, singing "Popular." Even Ms. Belfonte thought it was hilarious, Poppy said.

"Sounds fun," I said.

"Oh, it was," Poppy said. "How *was* tech rehearsal?"

"Okay. We banged on things."

"Sounds . . . loud," Avery said.

Minna wrapped her scarf around her neck. Carefully, so it wouldn't get caught on her brace. "Good for you, Wren. I'm totally hopeless at building."

"So am I," I said. "But I think I got the hang of it today. Mostly."

Poppy beamed. "Well, I'm just really, really glad Wren is doing the scenery, because then it'll be *beautiful*! And I can't *wait* to see what she does with the makeup!"

I winced. It sort of sounded like Poppy was doing an ad for me, like she was trying too hard to convince Avery and Minna.

Also, I couldn't help thinking Poppy was also reminding me to practice the Elphaba makeup. Which I hadn't been forgetting about, just kind of avoiding.

Then an even worse thing happened. Kai walked out of the auditorium, and froze right in front of us.

He looked at me. Nobody else, just me.

"*Oh,*" he said. His face went Magenta Magic. "Okay, well, see you tomorrow, Wren."

"Yeah, bye," I mumbled.

We watched him speed-walk out of the building, his arms crossed over his jacket, his chin practically touching his chest.

"Ooh, Wreeen, somebody liiiiikes you," Avery sang.

"Shut up, Avery," Poppy said. "It's not funny. And Wren can't help it if Kai likes her."

"Well, *I* think it's hilarious," Avery said.

Invitation

Every character is all about the eyes. The eyes tell you everything: emotions, backstory, secrets.

So this is what I always tell beginners: If you want to learn how to build character, concentrate on the eyes. Are they a special color? Are they open and bright? Do they have shadows and bags? Are the eyelids droopy, or heavy? Are the lashes long and lush, or thin? Or possibly fake? What about the eyebrows: Are they thick? Overplucked? Or iconic—like Spider-Man's or the Grinch's?

Seriously, guys, if you can afford only a few products, spend your money on eye stuff. Everything else can come later.

o O o

Tech crew met five times over the next two weeks. Henry and Pippa finished up the flat-building while Aliyah and I started painting the scenery: Madame Morrible's school, Elphaba's castle, the Ozdust Ballroom.

I'd never painted anything except our kitchen walls, but having a paintbrush in my hand felt comfortable. And not once did Kai try to correct my painting "technique." In fact, he pretty much ignored me, working with Ms. Chen and one of the computer teachers on the sound board. So I was starting to think maybe he didn't have a crush on me after all; maybe Avery—and I—had imagined the whole thing.

But then one day when I was rinsing the brushes, he walked over. He watched without saying anything as I wiped the bristles and added them to the bin where we kept supplies.

"Wren, can I ask you something?" he said finally. "Would you ever . . . I mean, if someone gave you a picture of a certain character's face, could you do the makeup for it?"

"Depends," I said. "Usually I just follow Cat FX's videos. But I can adapt things sometimes. Why?"

He glanced over his shoulder, like to check that no one was listening. "Remember I asked you about cosplay?"

I nodded.

"Well, there's this Comic Con coming up, and my dad's

getting tickets. So I was thinking of going as Thanos. Or maybe Daredevil or Iceman. I'm still deciding."

I thought for a few seconds. "Those are all so different. You like superheroes?"

"Yeah, I'm a big comics nerd. I especially like the Daredevil art by John Romita Sr. Even more than his Spider-Man stuff. But my favorite stuff you've probably never heard of. It's called *Wingz*. They all go through this portal into a dimension where everything is insect-themed?"

"You mean like Ant-Man? Or Black Widow?"

"Kind of. Although those characters have been stretched too far, in my opinion. I'm more interested in finite character arcs. But you hardly ever see pre-millennium comics with self-contained storylines anymore. Anyway."

I dried my hands on my paint-spattered smock. Kai talked like someone who spent all his time with his hobby. Although to him it probably wasn't a "hobby."

Kind of like me, actually.

"Well, yeah," I said. "I mean, I *might* be able to do those characters. But I'd need to do some research first."

Kai's eyes lit up. His two different-colored eyes. Although the rest of his face was just regular: olive skin, slightly crooked nose, sharp chin. Messy brown hair that stuck up, like he had permanent bedhead.

To do Kai's makeup, I'd have to touch his face. Of course,

if I was doing makeup for the show, I'd be touching Avery's face, and maybe others', too. Time to stop being so squeamish about this, really.

"What kind of research?" he was asking.

"YouTube," I said. "To see if there's a how-to video. I'm sure Cat FX never did those characters, but maybe someone else did. And I should know if there's any special products I'd need."

"Oh. Well, if you do need extra stuff, I could buy it. Or, rather, my dad will." He cleared his throat. "Also, Wren, you know, you could come to Comic Con with us. If you wanted."

I stared at him. "Seriously?"

"Yeah, my dad always buys multiday passes and an extra ticket so I can invite someone. But I never do." He stuck his hands in his pockets and stared at the floor tiles.

"Sure," I heard myself say. "I mean, thank you! When is it?"

"Not for a while. In the spring, at some big convention center in the city. I'll let you know the details, but it'll be around the same time as the play."

I had this feeling that he was about to say something else. So I jumped in first.

"Okay, well, thanks for the invitation, and I'll do that research on those characters, okay?" I said it too loud, with too many *okay*s. But at least it ended the conversation.

"Cool," Kai replied with a smile that was much too big.

Crush

As we walked home that day, Poppy talked about Emmett Brooker. How funny he was during rehearsal. What a great voice he had. How he'd shared his granola bar with her. What that meant. What did *I* think it meant?

"That he has good manners?" I said.

Poppy grinned. "Well, *sure* he does, Wren! But do you think it means anything *besides* that?"

"Like what?"

Her breath made a small cloud in the freezing air. "If I tell you something, you promise not to tell anyone else?"

"Of course."

"Soooo. Camila says she thinks Emmett has a crush on me."

"How would she know that?"

"*How?* She says it's obvious."

I thought about that word: "obvious." What made a crush "obvious" to other people? Was it when someone noticed your drawing, and remembered it for months afterward? Or kept talking to you, but always with a bunch of awkward silences? Or wouldn't stop blushing? Or invited you to Comic Con?

I mean, Avery acted like Kai's crush was a joke. But I knew it wasn't a joke; it was real. And Kai wasn't a joke either. Yes, he was awkward and also a know-it-all. But the truth was he *did* know a lot of stuff—not only about hammers and tech equipment but also about comics and superheroes. The two of us had *stuff in common*, hobbies that weren't just hobbies.

Except except except. Except I didn't have a crush *back*.

I wished I could talk to Poppy about what to do about the Kai situation. Could I get out of doing his cosplay makeup when I'd already said I would? Should I un-accept his invitation to Comic Con even though I really wanted to go? One thing I was sure of: I didn't want to hurt him. It was obvious he had even fewer friends than I did. And after the Annika business back in Abingdon, I knew how it felt to have zero.

I peeked at Poppy, who was still going on and on about Emmett and the dumb granola bar. She was someone who liked people and, poof, they liked her back. For her the social thing was brainless and automatic. Even if it sometimes meant "acting happy."

If I try to explain, she won't get it, I thought.

So who would, then?

Right away I knew the answer: Mom.

Ghost Eyes

A few minutes later I was home. No sign of Mom, so I took Lulu out for a quick walk and a long pee. Then I made myself some Swiss Miss and brought it upstairs to my room, where Cyrus was snoozing at the foot of my bed in the last little patch of afternoon sunlight.

I turned on my laptop.

First thing I checked, like always: Cat FX. But she hadn't uploaded anything for two days. Oh well. Probably she was busy with whatever she did in her non-makeup life.

I searched for Thanos and Iceman. No how-to videos, so I looked up images. Yep, these were effects I could do, and I already had most of the products. Which was good; I felt funny about asking Kai's dad to buy me things. Even if they were for Kai, not me.

I sipped my cocoa.

And typed: *two different color eyes.*

Heterochromia. A condition in which the iris is multi-colored. In some cases the iris of one eye may be a different color from the other. Usually heterochromia is benign, and does not affect vision. Very rare in humans but often seen in horses, dogs, and cats.

In folklore: In Native American cultures, heterochromia, referred to as "ghost eyes," is thought to give the possessor the ability to see into heaven. Eastern European pagan cultures considered heterochromia a sign that a newborn baby's eyes had been swapped with the eyes of a witch.

Whoa, I thought. *Does Kai know any of this?* If I told him I looked it up, probably he'd get the wrong idea about my interest.

But I had to admit it was extremely cool. Was there a superhero with heterochromia? Ghost Eye would be an awesome name, really.

The doorbell rang. Nobody ever rang our doorbell, so I didn't register it at first. But it kept ringing, so I ran downstairs to the kitchen.

"Who is it?" I asked.

"Wren, it's Krystal."

I opened the door and she came inside, not stopping to wipe her boots on the rubber mat. She was wearing a puffy black coat over bubble-gum-pink scrubs. Around her neck was a red scarf that looked hand-knitted.

Why was she here?

"Your mom home?" Krystal was smiling, but not with her eyes.

I shook my head.

"Any idea where she is?"

"I thought . . . she was at work."

"No, honey. She had a shift this morning and she never showed up. I tried to call her cell, but she's not answering."

I swallowed. "She does that sometimes. Doesn't answer her phone." *Yes, but when she's snoozing on the sofa. Which she isn't now, obviously.*

Krystal nodded, but not like she was agreeing. More like she was receiving information. "I didn't see her car out front. Any idea where she'd go?"

"Not really. She's always at the hospital."

Krystal's eyes stayed neutral. "She didn't leave you a note?"

"No. Usually she does, but sometimes she doesn't."

She nodded to show she'd received that information

too. I had the feeling right then that Krystal had practice keeping her face blank. Like if she saw scary things in the ER, she'd never alarm her patients.

She patted my arm. "Well, I'm sure there's a good explanation. Maybe your mom left her phone in the wrong bag. Or it ran out of juice. My son Tyndall's always forgetting where he put the charger, and it drives me crazy."

I didn't say anything.

"Anyhow," Krystal said. "So, when your mom shows up, could you ask her to give me a call?"

"Okay."

"Don't worry, Wren. I'm sure everything's fine. Your mom doesn't always communicate, but she knows how to take care."

Krystal opened her arms, inviting me for a hug. Even though it was a little awkward, I let myself be cocooned in her puffy black coat.

"You got everything you need here, Wren?" she asked softly. "Plenty of food for supper?"

Did I? And would Mom really be gone that long?

"Yeah," I said.

"All right, then. You have my number, honey." Krystal ended the hug. And then her voice was crisp again. Nurse-like. "And don't forget to have her call me. As soon as she gets home, all right?"

Personal

I didn't know what else to do, so I fed Lulu supper, filled her water bowl, and then went back upstairs to my room.

I sat on my bed. The patch of sunlight on my comforter had disappeared, but Cyrus was still sleeping, making old-cat sounds through his nose. I rubbed his head for a minute, but it didn't calm me down.

So even though I knew what would happen, I called Mom's cell. Of course it went to voice mail. I waited two minutes and called again. Still voice mail. Three minutes later, voice mail again.

I considered calling Dad. He'd told me to call him for "anything at all." Mom not showing up for work, not telling me—or Krystal—was definitely a reason to call. But what if she came home any minute with a perfectly logical explanation? Maybe her supervisor messed up again, and she didn't have a shift at the hospital after all, so she went to a movie and turned off her phone. Or something.

If I called Dad, I knew Mom would see it as me "talking behind her back." Also, once I called him, I wouldn't be able to un-call him. I figured Dad would keep asking questions, wanting updates about Mom. And then I'd have to report to him, like I was a spy. Or just lie, which I didn't want to do either.

I couldn't imagine Dad knew where Mom was anyway. Plus, he was a zillion miles away in Brooklyn. So he couldn't just pop over to go looking for her.

Although talking to him would calm me down, wouldn't it? And right now my heart was banging and my hands were so wet I had to wipe them on my jeans.

All right, so what if I just waited a little? If Mom showed up, everything would be fine, and Dad wouldn't even have to know.

I watched some old Cat FX videos: Nebula, Gamora, a unicorn, the Oldest Woman on Record, Person with a Black Eye. Shuri, the Grinch, Deadpool . . .

Seventy minutes. Seventy-two. My stomach felt like fireworks. Too jittery to even consider supper.

I checked the time: eight forty-five. Not crazy late if Mom was at the hospital.

Except she wasn't. Krystal had said.

Should I call Dad *now*?

Wait for one more video. The mermaid. Maybe if I looked super closely, I'd see what kind of pigment she was using for the face. Because Mom was right: even Cat FX could make a mistake with the product. Could she have misread the label? Not likely, but not impossible.

I hit Play.

> *Hey, guys, Cat FX here. Today I'm going to show you my favorite character of all time: the mermaid. This one is a total product of my imagination. And in my humble opinion, those are always the best effects, because you're not trying to copy someone's work. And every time you do the character, you can add some cool new variation—*

GGRRRRUUUNNNCHHH.

The garage door! My heart stopped. Then restarted.

I raced downstairs.

Mom came in the door with two shopping bags. She looked . . . okay. (Why did I think she wouldn't?) But tired. Wearing her scrubs.

Why is she wearing scrubs if she didn't go to the hospital?

"Hey, jellybean," she said, like *Ho-hum, here I am, back*

home after another day at the office. Except "jellybean" was Dad's nickname for me, not hers.

"Mom, where *were* you?" My voice sounded like an accusation. But I didn't care.

"What do you mean?" Mom started removing stuff from the shopping bags. Milk, oranges, aluminum foil, lettuce—

"You didn't go to work." My throat burned. "Krystal came over. She told me."

She stopped putting away groceries. "Krystal was here?"

"Yeah. She said you had a shift, but you never showed up."

"Well, that's just wrong. I *know* I told my supervisor—"

"And you didn't answer the phone all day. She said she called you a bunch of times, and so did I."

"Because I had terrible cell reception! And anyway, I couldn't talk."

"Why not? Why couldn't you talk?"

Mom reached into the shopping bag. She took out a box of Brillo and a jug of Tide. "Because I was busy. Wren, some grown-up things are just private, okay?"

"No," I said. Even though my throat felt scorched, my voice was too loud. "I'm not a baby, Mom. You have to tell me where you were!"

She shook her head. "Sweetheart, I just had to meet someone, okay?"

"Who? You mean like a boyfriend?"

"No, not a boyfriend."

"A *girl*friend?"

"Look, just someone I know. I don't want to talk about it, all right?"

We stared at each other.

"This is so unfair," I said. "You make *me* talk about *my* social life."

"Because it's my job as your mother! And besides, it's not my social life; it's just personal. Wren, *please* stop asking—"

"Oh, so if I don't want to talk about who I hang out with at school, or *if* I hang out, that's not okay, you can force me to do stuff I don't want to do and threaten to take away my computer, but *you* can disappear for hours, not even answer your phone, and I'm not allowed to ask who you're *with*?"

I'd never challenged her like this before. I'd never yelled at her either. We both stood there in shock, our eyes popping.

"Wren," Mom said. Her voice was shaky. "Why are you acting like this?"

I couldn't answer. I didn't know. Or maybe I did.

I burst into tears.

"Call Krystal," I said, and ran upstairs to my room.

148

Mask

I shut my door, but of course it didn't have a lock. Because why did bedroom doors need locks? They didn't.

About fifteen minutes later Mom opened the door and sat on my bed. Cyrus had jumped off a while ago, but now that Mom was on his turf, he was back. She rubbed her hand on his fur, and he began purring. How come she didn't want him on her bed, if she liked him so much?

Also, Mom had changed out of her scrubs. Maybe she'd decided there was no point still wearing a costume.

"Wren, I'm very, very sorry." Mom's voice was soft. "I know Krystal coming over must have really worried you. And I was wrong not to communicate; I should have left you a note. Or texted."

"And said what? 'I'm off somewhere I refuse to tell you about'?"

"Please, baby. I just had some personal business I needed to take care of. And I knew you didn't expect me to be home after school today, anyway."

"So if Krystal hadn't come over, I wouldn't even know about it, right?" My mind was racing. All those other times when Mom wasn't home after school, when I just assumed she was at work, was she even *at* the hospital? Or was she somewhere else, doing personal/private/grown-up things she didn't want to tell me about?

Mom gave a small, sad smile. "Listen to me, Wren. I apologize again if I made you worry. I honestly didn't think you would, but that wasn't fair of me, and I should have thought about it more clearly. And everything is fine, I promise."

She stood and held out her arms. I had no choice but to go hug her, so I did.

This close to her face, I could see she'd put on foundation. But she hadn't blended it, so the too-pink liquid had settled into the lines around her mouth, making her seem older and more tired. And with the purple shadows under her eyes, her face was a pink-and-purple mask.

Cat FX says masks hide the truth. Versus makeup, which reveals.

Why is Mom wearing a mask? Not even a good one.

Still hugging, still speaking softly, Mom said, "Wren,

honey? You didn't mention this to your father, right?"

That question again.

"Yeah, I didn't," I said. "Because it's not like I know anything anyway."

It was an angry thing to say, but I didn't care. I pulled away from the hug, went to my desk, and opened my laptop.

Mom sighed, went to her room, and locked her door.

Click.

Rey

Over the next three weeks, Mom worked afternoon shifts that went through supper and evening, plus overtime on the weekends. She worked so hard and for so many hours that she forgot to take me to the dentist, even though I'd reminded her like eighteen times about my appointment.

I mean, *probably* she was at work. Most afternoons when I got home from school, there was a note on the kitchen counter. Something like: *Mac and cheese in the fridge for dinner! I should be home around 8. Do your home-work.* ♥ ♥ ♥ And since Krystal wasn't calling, or coming over, to ask where Mom was, I had no reason to suspect she wasn't at the hospital. And anyway, when Mom got home, her scrubs looked wrinkled and sweaty, the way they did after a long shift.

But still, I couldn't help wondering.

One time when Dad called, he pointed out that spring break was only two months away, so he'd be getting my plane tickets pretty soon. But of course I could always visit before then—

"Can't," I told him. "I'm super busy. With the play."

This answer surprised even me. Mom was back (or seemed to be back) on a normal-for-her schedule, but I wasn't totally over her disappearance, and the way she'd told me not to "mention" any of it to Dad. So even though I wasn't angry at her anymore, I couldn't stop feeling that if I flew off to Brooklyn, the invisible strings tying me to Mom might snap completely. And then I wouldn't be able to come home at all. Not to Mom, Cyrus, Lulu, Poppy, and to the rest of my life here in Donwood.

The other possibility if I left: Mom would crash through the ceiling and float away. Actually, this seemed way more likely.

So I knew it wasn't logical, or even sane, but the truth was I was afraid to visit Brooklyn. Even for a quick snuggly weekend with the babies. And of course with Dad and Vanessa, too.

But at least I hadn't lied to Dad: the play really *was* keeping me busy. Now that the cast had moved to the auditorium for rehearsals, the tech crew met every afternoon in the art room, the gym, and sometimes the band room. We were still painting the flats for Elphaba's castle and the Ozdust Ballroom. Also, we'd begun constructing props—Nessa's wheelchair, Elphaba's hat, Glinda's wand, and a bunch of witch-hunting weapons.

Kai didn't ask about my research for his cosplay characters, and I didn't bring it up. For two reasons: First, because I knew he'd want to practice, and I wasn't super eager to meet after tech crew, just the two of us, to try out makeup effects on his face. (Where would even we do it? At school? I couldn't imagine him sitting at my desk at home, like Poppy.)

The second reason: I still felt squirmy about the Comic Con invitation.

Especially because he'd started giving me little presents. At first I didn't realize they *were* presents. Or that they were from *him*. Once after gym I found a little Rey action figure on my backpack, so I brought it to the Lost and Found.

A few days later, in math, there was one of those fancy charcoal art pencils on my desk, and when I held it up to ask whose it was (because I thought someone had left it there by mistake), Kai turned Magenta Magic. "No, no, it's for you, Wren," he said. "Yours to keep."

"But why?" I asked. I could hear how rude this sounded, but I couldn't help it.

"Because you draw stuff, right?"

Of course I did—but the thing was, Kai drew stuff too. In his notebooks during class, especially in math: complicated robots that transformed into other complicated robots. Or comic-booky villains with see-through heads and arms that shot thunderbolts.

Except he drew those in pen, so maybe he didn't need a fancy charcoal pencil? I thanked him to end the conversation.

And when he saw me using it to draw a 3D eyeball while Ms. Arroyo explained the Pythagorean theorem for the seventeenth time, he left two more pencils on my desk the next day.

"Kai, seriously, you shouldn't—" I began.

"No, it's fine," he said. "I got a whole box of these for Christmas from my uncle. And I never use them, so it's better if you have them for your character planning. Really."

Avery grinned at us. She made a heart shape with her hands, then leaned over and said something to Minna, who turned around to stare.

A week later Kai left a Daredevil comic on my chair. It was in one of those see-through plastic sleeves, like it was a rare special edition, a collector's item.

This was my limit.

I walked over to his desk to hand it back to him. "Kai, thank you, but I can't keep this," I said. I kept my voice quiet, but I tried to sound firm. The way I imagined Krystal would sound if she wanted a patient to take some awful-tasting medicine.

"It's not for you to *keep*," Kai said. "It's just for research. For the characters I was telling you about? I know there isn't a ton of stuff online, so I thought it might help you if—"

"All right," I interrupted. "Don't worry, I'll give it back tomorrow."

This time I was the one turning Magenta Magic. Because Avery was pointing at Kai and mouthing, *He liiiiikes you,* and Poppy's eyes were full of sympathy.

Skull

A few days later Ms. Belfonte said she wanted to rehearse with the leads only, so that meant Poppy was free after school for once. Ms. Chen had canceled tech crew to go to a faculty meeting or something, so I was free too.

At dismissal Poppy grabbed my arm. "Hey, Wren, wanna do a face today? I think a creepy skull would be so fun!"

I grinned. Finally I could be with Poppy, just the two of us, without Avery or Minna or anyone else. Cat FX had a skull video we could follow. Plus Mom would be at work today—she'd told me at breakfast—so we'd have the house to ourselves.

Of course I said yes.

The whole walk home, Poppy talked about the play: Avery was struggling with the high notes in "Defying

Gravity," but that eighth grader Gracie Ng was doing amazing with "Popular"! And Emmett Brooker—well, you know, *Emmett Brooker*. Omigod, the way he sang "As Long As You're Mine": "Maybe I'm brainless, maybe I'm wise / But you've got me seeing through different eyes. . . ."

Poppy sang loudly and so off-key it made my teeth hurt. *So Kai was right about her singing,* I thought.

And were love duets always this sappy? The lyrics were kind of embarrassing, really. Hard to imagine singing that onstage without giggling.

Of course, I didn't say this to Poppy.

When we got home, I took Lulu outside to pee and gave her a bully stick to chew, then asked Poppy if she wanted snacks.

"Obviously." She grinned. "Just like always."

I grinned back, because we had an "always." Except today the snack shelf was empty—none of that stuff Mom swiped from the nurses' station, the little packets of Oreos and Chips Ahoy and goldfish crackers that Poppy ate whenever she came over.

Crap. Why hadn't I noticed we'd run out of nurse snacks? And why hadn't Mom restocked the shelf? Or cleaned the kitchen counter, which was full of coffee stains and breakfast crumbs?

I searched for other options. "You want an apple? We have tons of peanut butter—"

"No thanks, Wren," Poppy said cheerfully. "I had a big lunch anyway."

Was she disappointed? I couldn't help wondering if she was hiding her feelings, "acting happy." Even with me.

We went upstairs. I peeked down the hall to see if Mom's door was shut. It wasn't, which was odd. She always kept it locked when she wasn't home.

"Everything okay?" Poppy asked.

"Yeah, fine," I said. "I was just thinking about the makeup." *And now I'm hiding my feelings too.*

Poppy plopped onto my bed next to Cyrus, who opened his one eye and went back to snoring. I started my computer and typed *Cat FX skull.*

We watched the video. Just as I remembered, the skull wasn't as tricky as the Giant Eyeball or even the mermaid. Nothing fancy or expensive, but still time-consuming and complicated, especially without practice.

"You sure you want to do this?" I asked Poppy. "It's in layers, so it won't be fast."

"I'm just a skeleton; I've got all day," Poppy replied. She got a towel from my bathroom to wrap around her shoulders while I fetched Vanessa's makeup kit from under my bed.

First I applied two layers of Clown White foundation all over her face. Then I defined the eye sockets and
cheekbones with black eyeliner and traced a triangle shape
around the tip of the nose. Like Cat FX said, the trickiest
part was the teeth, because you had to extend them beyond
the lips, and also show all the tooth roots. Plus, the skull
had to look 3D, so you needed to shade everything without smudging. Which was harder than it should have been
because Poppy wouldn't stop talking: *Emmett Brooker, Valentine's Day, blahblahblah.*

"How about you, Wren?" she asked as I added a few
cracks to the temples and jawline, just like Cat FX said.
"Are you giving a valentine to Kai?"

My hand dropped an inch. "What?"

"Oh, come on! You *know* he has a crush on you. Do you
have a crush on *him*?"

"Poppy, I can't do this makeup if you keep talking!"

"I mean, okay, he's a little weird. But incredibly smart,
don't you think?"

I painted some vertebrae on her neck. "Yeah, he is, and
a really good artist."

"You know," she continued, "you really shouldn't care
what Avery says. If *you* like Kai, that's *your* business, right?
And if you *do* want to give him a valentine—"

"Who says I do?" It came out too sharp, I could tell.

But why was everyone—including Kai—pushing me to like him? Why did I have to like *anyone*? Was this a seventh-grade thing? Or a Donwood thing? Nobody cared who I liked back in Abingdon.

And the truth was, I hadn't decided if I liked boys, or girls, or both. Or maybe no one at all.

"Okay, I'll shut up now," Poppy said, pretending to laugh a little, as if the whole valentine thing was just a joke.

For a minute she was quiet while I applied the final touches—mascara, and a hint of Magic Mauve on the eyelids.

Then her phone rang. She answered, holding it far enough from her face that it wouldn't get all white from the makeup. When she explained where she was, I could hear an impatient-sounding woman's voice: "Well, that sounds fun, but time to go home now. Olive's lonely, she needs help with homework, and I'm stuck here at the office—"

Poppy rolled her eyes at me. *My mooooom,* she mouthed.

Finally the call was over and Poppy slipped the phone in her pocket. "Sorry, Wren, gotta go hang with my little sister, because my big brother's too busy playing video games. Can you please get this stuff off my face really fast? Before Olive calls my mom again? Or the police?"

I reached for the makeup remover. But the bottle was

almost empty, and you needed tons of this stuff to remove all the white foundation, and also all the black.

Did I have any in the Mom shoebox? Only some nearly dried-up wipes. *Crap.*

"Is there a problem?" Poppy asked. She looked worried. I had a sudden thought: Mom's door was unlocked, so I could check her bathroom. She hardly wore any makeup, but enough that she'd need remover sometimes.

"One sec," I told Poppy. "Stay here, okay?"

I ran down the hall to Mom's bedroom. Her comforter was in a jumble, like she'd wrestled with it all night. Her dresser drawers were half-open, with socks and underwear hanging out. Pajamas on the floor, mug on the dresser, one-third full of coffee. How could she scold *me* about neatness when her own bedroom was such a mess? Plus the kitchen, too.

But her bathroom was spotless. Nothing around the sink except Dove soap, toothpaste, and a bottle of mouthwash.

So I opened the medicine cabinet.

Five unopened boxes of Band-Aids. Deodorant. Bacitracin. Dental floss. Her electric toothbrush. That awful too-pink foundation she wore. Moisturizer. Tylenol.

Also bottles.

Seven little orange bottles of pills. No labels.

Why does Mom have so many pills?

What are they for? Why aren't they labeled?

"Wren? Hurry up, I need to leeeave," Poppy was calling.

I grabbed the makeup remover and ran down the hall.

Bottles

Okay, you guys, this is important, so listen up: You almost never want to apply just one color, because if you do, it'll look flat and unrealistic. Most effects are about blending different shades—light, dark, and medium. That's how you get contours and dimension in your work.

And you know, nobody is just one color. People are messy. And they look different under different lights.

Mom came home that night at 7:48. It had been an extra-hard day in the ER, she said, so all she wanted was a bowl of chicken soup and Netflix.

I took Lulu outside for the evening pee. Then I snuggled next to Mom on the sofa while she slurped her soup.

"Can I please talk to you a minute?" I said. My heart was beating so loud I was sure she could hear it through my sweater.

"Of course." Mom put down the soup and looked at me with worried eyes. "Everything all right at school?"

"Yeah. It's not about school." I swallowed. "Please don't get mad at me, okay?"

"Wren, honey, when someone tells you not to get mad, it never works. What's wrong?"

Just say it. "Mom, you left your bedroom door unlocked. Poppy was here today, we were doing a skull, I ran out of makeup remover, and she had to leave—"

Mom jerked away and stared at me. "Wait. So you looked in my bedroom?"

"No. Your medicine cabinet."

Her face froze.

"Mom, why do you have so many pill bottles?" I asked.

She shook her head. Just kept shaking it, long past *No*.

"Mom? You haven't answered my—"

"Wrrreeennn," she said, as if she were trying out my name for the first time. "First of all, my personal medical stuff is my own business. You're old enough to respect that. And you shouldn't be snooping around in my bathroom."

"I wasn't snooping around! I was looking for *makeup remover*. Why aren't you answering my question?"

"I *am* answering your question, if you'd please just *listen*." She pushed her bangs out of her eyes. "Those pills are for my knee, all right? And for my back. And some are for sleeping."

"Okay. But why were there *so many*—"

She was shaking her head again. "Listen, sweetheart, this isn't something I want to discuss. I got them from the hospital, okay?"

I swallowed. "What does that mean, 'from the hospital'? You *took* them?"

I suddenly remembered what Mom had told me back in Abingdon, how her supervisor didn't trust her after a few pills "went missing."

"Honeybee, come on," Mom was saying. "You *know* nurses take home supplies *all the time*. Boxes of Band-Aids, those little packs of snacks you like—"

"But pills are different," I argued.

"They are? How?"

"Because they're medicine! They're dangerous! If you take too many—"

"But I wouldn't! I'm a nurse, remember? I *know* about these things; it's my job, which I happen to be *very good at*. Ask Krystal." She pressed her lips. "Besides, I've already seen a doctor about my knee. Two doctors, in fact. And I've had three MRIs. So unless I want surgery, which I absolutely do *not*, I have no choice but to treat my knee pain with meds."

"You have a knee doctor?"

"An excellent orthopedist at the hospital, okay? So don't worry." She picked up her bowl of soup and took a spoonful. "And, Wren?"

"Yeah?" I said. Already I was feeling better. I even smiled a little.

She looked at the TV, not at me. "Next time stay out of my bathroom," she said.

The Box

Hey, I know I tell you a million different steps for each character. And I usually recommend a ton of products, right? For some of you, that's cool. But I never want anyone to feel overwhelmed. So here's a secret message especially for you beginners: To get a great character going, you don't need to follow every single thing I say. If what I'm doing seems like too much, just pick a few details. And always focus on the eyes!

Vanessa hadn't sent a makeup package in a long time—nothing since before Christmas, in fact. I told myself it was understandable: She'd already sent so much stuff, and now she was busy with the babies. Plus, she and Dad had given me money for Chanuk-mas, so she probably figured I'd just buy my own supplies.

But one day the second week in February, when I got home from school after tech crew, Mom was sitting at the kitchen table with her red mug. She was wearing her lavender fleece bathrobe over pajamas, like she'd just gotten out of bed. In front of her was a small cardboard box, all taped up. With a typed label. Addressed to me.

My stomach dropped.

"Hey, honeybee," Mom said, watching as I took off my jacket. "How was school?"

"Okay." I kept my eyes away from the box. Maybe if I did, it would disappear. "You just woke up?"

"No, I'm off today, so I've been resting my knee. How was tech crew?"

"Pretty good. We're almost done with the scenery."

She pointed to the box. "Looks like you have mail. What is it?"

The return address said XYZ Cosmetix from somewhere in Arizona. Right away I recognized the name; Vanessa had ordered from them once before.

"I'm not sure," I said.

Mom cocked her head. "You ordered something, but you don't know what? With my credit card?"

"No, no." My face was burning. "I think it's from Dad, actually."

"Really? Well, why don't you open it."

I was trapped; I couldn't just grab the box and open it in my room, with my door closed, the way I usually did when something showed up in the mail.

While Mom sipped from her mug, I took a small knife from the counter and carefully sliced the packing tape. About a square foot of bubble wrap surrounded a tiny jar of witch-green pigment.

"And there's a note," Mom said.

"It's nothing."

"It's not *nothing*; it looks like a gift message. What does it say?"

I had no choice but to read it out loud. "'Dear Wren, I hope this green is the one you wanted. I'm sure you'll create a beautiful Elphaba. Please take many photos!! We love you and are so proud of your art. V.'"

"V is Vanessa? She ordered this for you?" Mom asked.

I nodded.

"Does she . . . send you stuff often?"

"She used to. But not in a very long time."

"Oh." Mom raked her bangs and blinked a few times. "You never told me, Wren."

"Well, you're always at work when I get the mail."

"Not *every day*. And even if I was at work, you could mention it when I got home."

"Mom, it's not a big deal; it's just makeup stuff! And

you're always so tired and grumpy after work; I didn't think you'd want to hear about it!"

Mom's face had that frozen look. She didn't say anything.

"It's only for the play, anyway," I said. Now my voice was squeaking. "Ms. Belfonte said we're on a tight budget, and I told Dad and Vanessa, and they wanted to help out. Vanessa's into art supplies. It's not a big deal," I repeated.

"It's a big deal that you lied to me," Mom said.

"But I didn't! I just didn't *tell* you because I thought you wouldn't want to hear!" Suddenly I was crying so hard that my mouth was full of tears. "Mom, I know you're mad at Dad, I understand all that, but Vanessa's just trying to be nice, I like her, and I really hate it that I can never say her name around you! Or talk about the babies! Or even Dad!"

Mom's eyes went dark and flat, like smooth black stones. I tried to read behind them, but I couldn't get past the dark flatness.

After a minute, she got up from the table, put her mug in the sink, and went upstairs to her bedroom.

CLICK.

All night I listened for a loud shouting phone call down the hall, but I didn't hear a thing.

Violets Are Blue

Mom didn't get up to have breakfast with me the next morning, and I definitely wasn't going to wake her. I knew she felt mad at me, betrayed, because I'd said that Vanessa was a nice person and not a Wicked Stepmother, or a home wrecker, or anything cartoon-villainy like that. And of course also because she'd been sending me packages. Which I hadn't told Mom about.

Why hadn't I? Of course I should have. It was wrong and stupid to keep it a secret from Mom, who always found out everything anyway.

So, yeah, I was mad at me, too.

But also: I couldn't stop thinking about what Cat FX said about effects makeup, how the colors were never just one shade, but a messy blend. My feelings that morning were also a messy blend: shame, worry, frustration, sadness, and anger, plus a bunch of other colors too. Why had Mom walked out on our conversation, shutting me out of her bedroom? It was like she wanted me to tell her everything, share everything—but when I *did* try to talk to her, she locked her door on me. Like she couldn't deal with my messy feelings.

I ate my almost-burnt breakfast bagel, took Lulu out to pee, then left for school. I wasn't Mom's alarm clock, I told myself; if she was late getting to work again, that was her problem, not mine. Although I didn't even know if she had work today. It wasn't like she'd told me her schedule for the week.

And this was Valentine's Day, so I had other things on my mind. Last night Poppy had texted me her three ideas for a valentine for Emmett: a box of chocolate-covered teddy-bear gummies, a box of heart-shaped Red Hots, or a box of peppermints with sayings on them like WE'RE MINT FOR EACH OTHER.

Not the mints, I texted back. Tbh they sound dorky.

Aww, I like them, Poppy replied. And valentines shd be dorky. You'll see. She added the wink-and-tongue-sticking-out face.

Poppy's teasing made my stomach bounce. If Kai intended to give *me* some sort of dorky valentine, I needed a plan, I told myself. Not to be rude, just to let him know

I wasn't crush material, I wasn't interested, I didn't want peppermints or heart-shaped anything wrapped in red-and-pink foil.

Truthfully, it was hard to imagine him buying any of that stuff anyway. But what if he had? After that fight with Mom, I was still pretty shaky, in no mood for another messy talk about feelings.

No thank you, I practiced in my head. *Thank you, Kai, it's very nice of you, but NO THANKS.*

Weirdly, though, nothing showed up on my desk all day. Or on my backpack. Or next to my locker. Poppy got a single flower (a poppy!) from someone who'd attached a card signed *Your friend???* Minna got a bunch of cherry lollipops tied up with pink ribbon; nobody knew who sent them until Mateo admitted it was him. Avery brought chocolate cupcakes with pink sprinkles for the whole class, but if you wanted one, you had to walk over to her desk and ask, so I didn't. As for Emmett, he got a million valentines—cards and candy, including Poppy's box of dorky peppermints, which he shared with all his friends.

If Kai got a valentine from someone, I didn't see. Maybe somebody slipped him one in secret. But I doubted it.

Finally it was time for tech crew. Pippa and Aliyah were both wearing red everything—red sweaters, red skirts, red leggings, and red socks. Ms. Chen had brought us all little goody bags of gummy worms and conversation hearts that said DREAM BIG and WAY TO GO and JUST B U— nothing romantic, but they were still counted as Valentine's candy. And Kai kept peeking at me and blushing.

Seriously, I couldn't wait for this day to be over.

And it almost was. We'd just finished painting the last flat—the wall of Madame Morrible's academy—when Kai walked over and handed me a paper.

A drawing of Nebula. An incredibly detailed one, done in pen, with all the parts of her cybernetic eye.

At the bottom of the page was a poem written in letters so tiny you almost needed a magnifying glass:

> Roses are red
> Violets are blue
> Nebula's cool
> And so are you.

My hands dripped icy sweat. *Is this a valentine? It has to be: It says "Roses are red, violets are blue"! You only write that when it's a valentine!*

"What do you think?" Kai asked.

"It's a really good drawing," I said. "Except . . . violets aren't blue."

"What?"

"They're purple. Although 'purple' can mean lilac, orchid, mauve, iris, plum, raisin, eggplant—"

"Okay," Kai interrupted.

"And 'blue' is generic too. You should specify what blue you're talking about: indigo, cornflower, cobalt, steel, sky—"

"I *get* it, Wren," Kai said. "But what do you think about . . . the rest of it?"

"Well, it's an excellent Nebula. You drew the eye better than me. And I like how you did the top of her head."

"That's not what I meant."

He looked at me. *Heterochromia. Ghost eyes.*

"Kai, is this a valentine?" My voice was practically a whisper.

He shrugged. "I don't know. Maybe. I guess."

Just say it. Thank you but no thank you! "Well, I'm very sorry, but I can't. I mean, you're a nice person, Kai, I think you're smart and an incredibly good artist, I really like you, but I don't—"

Kai's ghost eyes filled with tears. He snatched the damp paper out of my hands and speed-walked out the door.

Emily

At least I made it home without crying. But as soon as I walked into the kitchen, forget it. I cried so loud, Lulu hobbled over to sit on my foot. This was comforting, but what I needed was a hug from Mom. Was she even home? And if she was, was she still mad at me from yesterday?

I wiped my face on a sour-smelling dish towel and followed a muffled sound coming from the living room. The TV was on, and there was Mom, snoring on the sofa, her bad knee curled around Cyrus. Who for some reason was not allowed in her bedroom.

I burst into tears all over again.

Mom sat up, blinking. "Wren? Come here, baby. What happened?"

I told her everything—about Kai's drawing, the poem, all the little presents, Avery's teasing. How he had no friends at school except me, and now, on Valentine's Day, I'd broken his heart.

"Oh, honeybee, hearts are way stronger than that." Mom kissed my wet cheek. "And they usually heal pretty fast. Trust me, I've seen enough hearts in the ER to know about this."

"But Dad broke your heart, right?"

Mom took a second before she answered. "Well, yes, he did."

"And you're all healed now?"

"That's a tough question, sweet girl. I think I'm still in the process of healing. Anyhow, one thing I've learned this past year is that we're all responsible for our own hearts. If someone does break ours—and I doubt you've actually broken this boy's—it's up to us to figure out a way forward."

She stroked my hair. I hiccupped. We stayed that way through two commercials.

Mom forgives me, I thought as I breathed in her familiar smell. *And I forgive her.* Although the truth was I'd lost track of what for.

She took my hand in a hand sandwich. Then she said, "Oh, by the way. I hired a housecleaner. She came today while you were at school and did some vacuuming."

"A housecleaner?"

"Yes, a nursing student. Named Emily. She'll probably come back in about a month."

"Okay." We'd never had a cleaner before, but we could use some extra help around here, actually.

Mom's phone rang. She picked it up from the coffee table. "Oh no," she said, staring at the screen.

I peeked: it was Krystal. "Mom, aren't you going to answer?"

She chewed her lower lip. Then she started talking. "Hey, Krystal. No, no, I know, I'm on my way. . . . She is? What did she say . . . ? Crap. Okay, well, can you please tell her I'm having car trouble again . . . ? Yeah. I don't know, like twenty minutes? I'm just out the door now. . . . Yeah, thanks, hon. Bye."

Mom put her phone down.

"Mom?" I said. "Is everything—"

"No, it's not. I was positive today was off! My supervisor keeps messing up my schedule."

I studied her face, which seemed like it had too much skin. She had purple shadows under her eyes. *No, not purple: mauve.*

"Maybe you should call in sick?" I said. "You do look sort of pale."

"I can't. If I stay home, I'll get fired."

"No you won't! You're a good nurse—"

"Thanks, sweetheart. Anyhow, I'll be fine." She got up from the sofa slowly, stiffly. "I need to get ready for work, okay? If my phone rings, don't answer."

She hobbled upstairs to her bedroom. I stayed on the sofa with Cyrus, worrying that Mom's boss was mad at her, and wondering what Mom meant about having car trouble "again."

A few minutes later, Mom was back downstairs in her spearmint scrubs, giving me instructions for dinner. She was wearing that too-pink foundation, which she'd obviously applied in a hurry, because she hadn't covered her nose or her jawline or all of her chin. I would have said something about how bad it looked, except she was already late for work.

"Wren, you sure you're feeling better now?" she asked as she grabbed her jacket and her bag.

"Yeah," I said. "Just go, Mom. Don't worry about me."

"God, I've always hated Valentine's Day." She blew me a kiss.

A few seconds later I heard the GGRRUUNNCCHH of the garage door, and she was gone.

That was when I realized I'd forgotten Lulu, so I got her leash and took her outside for a quick, careful walk up and down our icy block. Then I fed her some kibble and made myself a cheddar cheese sandwich (still no nurse snacks on the shelf). Mom never liked when I ate in my room, but since she wasn't here to scold, I brought the sandwich upstairs.

After this long, horrible day, the only thing that would make me feel a little better was doing some makeup. So I reached under my bed for the Chanuk-mas makeup case.

But it wasn't where I always kept it—flush against my headboard, by the wall.

I started to panic. Then I remembered about Emily. She must have moved it by accident when she vacuumed. I groped under the bed, brushing against several dust bunnies (this Emily wasn't much of a vacuumer!). Finally my fingers reached the case's edge by the foot of the bed.

My heart banging, I pulled it out and opened it on my bed.

Vanessa's makeup was there, exactly how I'd arranged it—lipsticks, pigments, eye shadows, creams, and brushes, all in separate compartments.

But the gift from Dad and Vanessa—two hundred dollars!—was gone.

Queen of Hearts

can't tell you how I spent the next few minutes. My brain was a jumble from today—nerves, tears. Comfort, worry. More tears. And now shock.

The money is gone because Emily stole it. What else made any sense? The new housecleaner must have vacuumed under my bed (although, considering all the dust bunnies, "vacuumed" wasn't the right word), found the makeup case, opened it, and stuck my money in her pocket! We should call the police! Or, since Mom said Emily was a nursing student, we should tell someone at the hospital! Maybe that supervisor of Mom's.

At the very least, I should definitely tell Mom. She should know that this Emily she hired was a thief, shouldn't she?

I sat on my bed with my cheese sandwich, my brain spinning in a hundred bad-weird directions.

I'll think about this later, I told myself.

Finally I tossed the sandwich, turned on my laptop, and watched Cat FX do the Queen of Hearts.

Jumpy

I decided to wait for the right moment to talk to Mom about the money. The timing was important, I knew. Because if I said that I suspected Emily, Mom would ask a million questions: Why had I told her that Vanessa had sent "a few things," when actually it was *a whole makeup case* of stuff? How long had I been hiding this makeup case—and all those products—under my bed? Was I ever planning to tell her about them? And also about, oh yes, *the money*?

Thereby starting a whole new fight about Dad and Vanessa.

But of course I had to say something—and soon, before this Emily person came back for another "cleaning."

So a few days later, when I came home from school to find Mom on the sofa, reading her phone, I snuggled next to her.

"Mom? Can I tell you something?" I said.

She looked up from her texts. "Of course, sweetheart."

"I think that cleaner you hired—Emily—stole my money."

I felt Mom's body stiffen. "What money?"

"My Chanuk-mas money. From Dad. I kept it under my bed so it wouldn't get lost. And now it's missing." I said all this fast, without breathing.

Mom didn't answer. Which was actually the *last* thing I expected.

"Mom?" I said.

"Well, that's just awful," she said after a few seconds. "I'm so disappointed in Emily. Obviously, I'll never hire her again."

And then she typed something into her phone.

Besides the missing money, the other big thing on my mind was Kai. Now that he barely grunted if I said hello, shrugged if I said I liked his drawing, and ignored me during tech crew, I felt terrible. Because I couldn't stop thinking that Kai was more *like* me than anyone else I knew, including Poppy. If he hadn't given me that stupid valentine, I wouldn't have hurt him. But he did, and I did. And now he hated me.

At school it was like everyone was onstage all the time. No one could hide, even the tech people. So of course everyone noticed Kai's behavior, including Avery, who asked at lunch one day if Kai and I had had "a lovers' quarrel."

"That's not funny, Avery," I snapped. "Anyhow, it's none of your business."

"But, Wren, we're all *dying* to know!" she said in the sort of bright, loud voice she probably used for Elphaba. Which meant the whole cafeteria could hear. "So you absolutely *have* to tell us! Is Kai mad because you forgot your nerdiversary? And you didn't send nerdflowers?"

"Shut up, Avery," Poppy said. She caught my eye.

Kai was sitting at the next table by himself, as usual. Staring at his phone, pretending not to hear.

"Oooh, wait, I know," Avery continued. "You asked Kai to the Nerd Prom, right? And he said no, he wasn't allowed out after dark unless he got a ride in his daddy's nerdmobile. So then *you* said—"

"*Shut up.*" I stood. My face was hot. "Why are you so mean, Avery? And so *boring*?"

"Okay, Wren," Poppy said, shooting me a look. "Avery is just teasing—"

"Well, I'm sorry, but it isn't funny," I said. "Kai is cool, and I refuse to listen to any more of Avery's garbage."

To be honest, I was a little shocked at myself. I peeked at Kai to see what he thought about my speech, but he'd already fled the cafeteria.

o O o

That night Poppy called. She didn't ask if this was a good time to talk; she just started talking.

"Wren, you should really apologize to Avery," she told me.

"Wait, seriously? Why?" I asked. "Because *she* insulted *me*. Also Kai."

"I know; I was there, remember? She was teasing and she definitely went too far. Sometimes she does that. But *you* kind of lost it too."

I couldn't believe Poppy was saying this. "You think I overreacted? Because you *saw* how she humiliated us! In front of everyone!"

"Hey, I'm agreeing with you, okay? Avery was wrong. But I think you made it worse." She paused. "Wren, is everything all right?"

"What do you mean?"

"I don't know. You seem a little . . . distracted lately. Jumpy."

"It's just some stuff with my mom," I said.

"Oh." She sounded surprised. "You want to talk about it?"

"Not really." I felt bad saying this. But Poppy's family had a house with solid floors, permanent ceilings. How much would she even understand?

Poppy sighed into her phone. "Well, I'm sorry that's happening, I really am. But trust me, you do *not* want Avery turning everyone against you. I've seen her do it to people. It won't be fun."

So in other words, Annika all over again. And then maybe we'll have to move!

"Also," Poppy continued, "you and Avery have to work together on Elphaba's makeup, right? If you guys are fighting, it'll be bad for *everyone*. So just tell Avery you had other stuff on your mind, you took it out on her, and you're sorry. Okay? Please."

I didn't say anything.

"Wren? You there? Oh no, did this call drop?"

"No, I'm here," I said.

Control

That night I couldn't sleep. I kept thinking about what Mom had said to me after the Annika disaster—*If you don't share your feelings, they have a way of coming back to bite you in the butt.*

Except was that always true? Was it better to give another big speech, telling Avery exactly how I felt, or to keep my mouth shut and apologize, the way Poppy wanted? Of course, not apologizing probably meant the fight with Avery would just keep snowballing into something worse. And even though I suspected Poppy wanted the fight to end mostly because she felt stuck in the middle, I also knew she wanted to protect me.

So, okay, fine, I'd apologize. Because I'd been through that hazardous-waste business with Annika, and I definitely didn't want zero friends again.

But still.

Why did I never have control over things? It felt like my only options ever were: Keep everyone happy. End the fighting. Don't make problems for other people.

Hide stuff under the bed.

Don't accuse anyone. Don't confront anyone.

Don't talk behind anyone's back.

Don't visit Brooklyn. Don't even talk about visiting Brooklyn.

Don't ask questions. Don't make things awkward.

Don't stick up for myself.

Pretend everyone and everything is fine.

Maybe someday I'd explode, or go crazy. Right now, though, I was just tired, sick of feeling this way. But also too . . . what was Poppy's word? Jumpy. Too jumpy to sleep. Even cuddling Cyrus didn't help.

So when the garage door grunched open at two a.m., I was awake to hear Mom clomp up the stairs, race into her bedroom (where she didn't bother locking the door), make it to her bathroom, and barf, over and over.

Mom stayed in bed the next day. A stomach bug, she said, her voice sounding weak through her closed door. And no, she didn't need anything besides rest, thanks. And quiet, please.

I went to school and apologized to Avery in front of Poppy.

"Yeah, okay," Avery muttered. "I'm sorry too."

She said it like a robot, preprogrammed and flat. And when Poppy beamed at me, I could tell she'd called Avery to make her apologize, just like she'd called me. But at least I wasn't the only one apologizing.

When I got home that afternoon, Krystal was sitting in the kitchen with Mom, who was wearing her bathrobe. Looking awful, like a cross between Creepy Broken Doll and Person with a Bad Cold.

"Just checking on the patient before work," Krystal said, winking at me.

"You really didn't have to," Mom told her. "And now that Wren's home, you should go, Krystal. I don't need us both getting fired."

"No one's getting fired," Krystal said scornfully. "Kelly, just go to bed, and I'll tidy the kitchen a little. Scoot." She flicked her hands at Mom, who went upstairs like an obedient child.

"Thanks, but you don't have to clean," I told Krystal.

"Well, *somebody* needs to." Krystal was already turning on the faucet. "This kitchen is a mess."

I looked around. She was right: There were dirty dishes in the sink, and crumbs on the counters and the floor. The overflowing garbage can gave off a sour smell, plus there was a separate odor (old garlic? old meat?) coming from the fridge.

How long had the kitchen been like this? And why hadn't I noticed?

Seriously, though, what was wrong with me? I could detect the teeniest makeup details—microscopic trails of powder on someone's jawline, the extremely subtle difference between Thin Ice Blue and Stone Cold Blue eye shadow. But when it came to what was right in front of me, the way our kitchen looked (and smelled), sometimes it was like my brain crashed. Or switched to a different video.

"You know, Wren, you're old enough to be helping out around here," Krystal was scolding as she added a plate to the dish rack. "Your mom works so hard, and when she comes home, she shouldn't be doing all the housework."

"But I do help," I said. "I clean all the time! And last week Mom hired Emily from the hospital to help us, but I think she'll hire someone else next time."

"Who's Emily?"

"A nursing student?"

"Huh. I don't know any nursing student named Emily. You sure that's her name?"

I shrugged. I was positive Mom had said her name was

Emily. But I'd been so upset about the Kai business it was possible I'd heard it wrong.

Krystal kept scrubbing a dish. "Anyway, I wanted to talk to you about something. Your mom's *not* getting fired, okay? She's an excellent nurse, we're short-staffed, and the patients love her. But our boss isn't crazy about all the phone calls."

"What phone calls?"

"The ones from you, honey."

"From me?"

"Yeah. Whenever you call, Kelly always drops everything to go chat in private. You know you're her top priority. But when she's at work, the interruptions are a problem. So from now on you need to call her only when it's *important*. Talk about the rest when she gets home. All right? Can you do that, honey?"

I told her I could. Of course I could.

Don't ask questions. Don't make things awkward.

Don't defend yourself.

"Good girl," Krystal said. "I knew I could count on you. Now why don't you wipe the counters and throw these smelly dish towels in the wash. I'll take out the garbage."

She dried her hands, blew me a kiss, and left for the hospital.

Jagged Glass

After Krystal left, my brain swirled in a million bad-weird directions.

Mom told Krystal I keep calling her at work?

Why would she say that?

Who is she talking to instead of me? The same person she was meeting when she disappeared?

As for Emily: Did I get her name wrong?

Does she even exist?

Why would Mom make up a story like that?

And if Emily wasn't here last week, who searched my room?

Under my bed?

Was it Mom?

Who else could it be?

So then did she—?

Why would she—?

And then lie about—?

What is going on with—?

Each question was like a jagged piece of glass that cut me on the inside.

The Money

Mom stayed home for two days, mostly behind her locked door. The few times she came downstairs, she looked terrible. When I hugged her once, her skin felt cold and clammy, and she smelled different. I couldn't say how, exactly, but it wasn't her usual soapy smell.

"Don't hug me; I'm probably contagious," she grumbled, pulling away.

But on the third morning she was completely fine. Fine for the next three weeks, in fact. So fine I wondered if I'd hallucinated the whole Emily business, and also the business about me calling her at the hospital.

I mean, I knew my Chanuk-mas money was missing. Also that someone had found the fancy makeup case under my bed. Those were facts. But all the details *around* those facts? Maybe they weren't how they seemed. Or maybe I was thinking about them the wrong way.

Because if it was *Mom* who'd found the makeup case, and also the money, how come she'd never said a word about it? Never confronted me, or even asked questions? None of that made any sense. And seriously, you'd think she be upset about me hiding stuff, especially after she found that package from Vanessa.

Now that she was fine again, I told myself that *me* bringing up this subject, all those jagged-glass questions and accusations, was a stupid idea. Why cause a fight when things were calm? Talking about the under-the-bed stuff meant going down a dangerous road, saying things we couldn't unsay. I was tired of worrying about everything. All I wanted was for home to be normal, predictable, boring. And now it was.

So when Dad flew out for a business trip to Chicago, and stopped in Donwood to take me out for a semifancy dinner, I chattered about nothing: We'd started rehearsals with the set in place. I'd failed my math test but could take a do-over. Lulu had gotten her shots. Cyrus needed a tooth cleaning.

Things were fine in Brooklyn, too, Dad said. Both babies were sitting now, and Ayla was rolling over from her back to her tummy! Vanessa had given up on the waterscapes and was painting sand dunes now. She was going crazy, though, trying to hire a nanny so she could return to work.

"And how's Mom?" Dad asked as he sliced his steak.

Home is good. Keep it that way, I told myself.

"Like usual. Busy at the hospital," I said.

Dad chewed for a few seconds. "I'm asking because she isn't returning my calls."

"She's not?"

"No, and she's never done that before. So I'm wondering what's up."

I dipped a ravioli in a small puddle of sauce. "I think it's because her boss doesn't allow phones at work."

"Really? That's strange." Dad frowned.

"Yeah, so the nurses don't get distracted. It sounds like her boss is really strict about that."

"Well, Mom and I need to discuss some scheduling stuff about your spring break. Although that's my problem, Rennie, not yours." Dad sliced more steak. "Speaking of scheduling, Vanessa and I were thinking about coming to your show."

"You mean *Wicked*? No, don't," I blurted.

"Why not?"

"Because Mom will be there, and it'll be weird for her.

Anyhow, I'm only doing makeup for this one character. You guys don't need to fly out here with the babies just for that! I'll send photos."

Dad's face fell. I knew I'd hurt his feelings, but I couldn't help it. The thought of Mom meeting Vanessa and possibly the babies on opening night—seriously, I had too many other worries.

"Well, I want you to know we're really proud of you, jellybean," Dad said. "*Both* of us."

"Both" meant Dad and Vanessa. Not Dad and Mom. Obviously.

I nodded. "I know you are, Dad. Thanks."

He wiped his mouth with a semifancy napkin. "On that topic, Vanessa told me to ask if you needed more makeup."

"*No.*" It came out too strong; Dad's eyebrows rose. "I mean, no *thank you*," I added. "I already have a ton."

"You don't need anything for the show?"

Do I? Ugh. I really need to get focused on Elphaba's makeup. I shook my head.

"What about the money?" he asked.

I went cold. "What money?"

"That Chanuk-mas gift we gave you, Rennie. Did you spend any of it yet? Buy yourself something nice?"

"It's *Wren*, Dad! Mom always remembers my name! Why can't you?"

Dad's eyes clouded. "Sorry, jellybean. I guess when you're used to seeing people a certain way, or calling them a certain name, it's hard to let go. But you're not a baby anymore. I need to remember better."

"It's okay," I said quickly. "Sorry for snapping at you."

He reached across the table for a hand sandwich. We sat like that for a while, not talking, until my hand started to sweat, so I pulled it away to wipe it on my napkin.

"Anyhow, I'm still thinking about the money," I said.

Spotlight

O ne day in the middle of March, Ms. Belfonte called me to the auditorium. "I'd like to see Elphaba under the lights," she said. "And for Avery to get comfortable in the makeup. Can you meet after school tomorrow for a practice run?"

"Wait, you mean *do* the Elphaba makeup? On Avery?" My voice squeaked.

Kai was standing behind Ms. Belfonte, typing on his phone. He looked up.

Our eyes met.

He frowned and looked at his phone.

"That's right," Ms. Belfonte said. "Opening night is just three weeks away! So at this point it would help Avery—and the whole cast, actually—for Elphaba to look like Elphaba."

"Sure, no problem," I said.

And then I ran out of the auditorium, yelling at myself the whole way home. Why hadn't I been practicing Elphaba's makeup? Poppy had tried to get me to focus, but I'd just kept putting it off. Mostly because of Avery, how mean she was, especially about Kai. Seriously, though, I had to stop being such a baby! Professional makeup artists had to work with all sorts of people! And anyhow, Avery had apologized. Even if Poppy had forced her.

But I couldn't stop thinking how, once again, my brain had shut off. Avoided something that was hard, or messy, or complicated.

Why did I keep doing this? What was wrong with me?

Well, at least this problem wasn't too late to fix! All I had to do was follow Cat FX's instructions. Layer by layer, step by step. I'd done it a million times, for a million other characters, and I could do it for Elphaba, too.

And just imagining Cat FX's cheery voice comforted me: *Hey, guys, Cat FX here . . .*

Other than myself, the only people I'd ever done makeup for were:

Vanessa (although just cat eyes, which were
technically not a special effect, so didn't count)

Annika (although she'd freaked before I could finish)

Mom (who didn't count, because *of course* I was fine touching her face, and also *of course* she'd think everything I did was great)

Poppy (my best friend, so obviously she'd say nice things)

I knew it made sense that I was scared to do Avery. Not only because she was Avery-who-judged-and-teased-me. Also because she was *another person* on this very short list. Whose makeup happened to be the most important effect in the entire show.

But what I didn't expect was that the next day, when we met in the band room, Avery would be scared too.

"You've done Elphaba before, right?" she asked as I set up the supplies on a small table.

"Not a lot," I admitted. "Just on my mom once. But I've done other characters."

"With Poppy, right? She says you're really good at this."

Poppy talks about me? To Avery?

"Thanks," I said, trying to sound casual.

My hands were trembling as I brushed on some powder, then applied foundation to even out her skin tone. Avery's skin was much darker than Cat FX's or Mom's; I'd have to figure out how to build up the green to make it just right for her. And would I be able to do eyeliner and lipliner, make straight, clean lines with these jittery fingers? I didn't see how it was possible.

And the thought of this—of messing up Elphaba, making Avery hate me even worse—made my palms so wet I could barely grip the brush. So finally I gave up on it and just used my damp pointer finger to blend the foundation.

Avery flinched. "Your hands are really cold, Wren. And clammy."

Uh-oh, here it comes. "Sorry."

"I'm not criticizing. So are mine. They always freeze when I get nervous. See?"

She touched my wrist with icy fingers.

"Why are you nervous?" I asked.

"Ugh." Avery rolled her eyes. "Because I *hate* how I look in makeup."

"Same. But think of it this way: I'm not doing *your* makeup. I'm doing Elphaba's."

Avery didn't argue with that, but I could tell she stayed nervous. She kept licking her lips as I brushed on layers of green face paint, then used my fingers to contour the cheekbone, jawline, and hairline with Vanessa's Magic Mauve. She blinked while I redefined her brows with black eye shadow and applied Royal Purple shadow to her eyes.

And she twitched when I outlined her lips in Vampire Kiss Purple, filling them in with Loch Ness Green.

But the funny thing was, the more I did, the calmer I felt. Especially because—unlike Poppy, who wouldn't shut up—Avery didn't say a word. No chatter about boys, but also no teasing or snarky comments. No complaining about how long the makeup was taking either. And with Cat FX's voice in my head, coaching me every step of the way, I could zone out and just focus on the work. Although between steps I still worried about Avery's reaction.

When I finally finished, about twenty minutes later, I handed her a mirror, half expecting her to shriek like Annika.

Except she didn't. She just looked at herself for a minute, turning her head from side to side, popping her eyes, stretching her mouth, lifting her chin.

"Okay if I try singing?" she asked.

"Sure," I said. Shrugging like, *Yeah, actors ask me for permission to sing all the time.*

Avery took a deep breath. "Something has changed within me. / Something is not the same. . . ."

She closed her mouth and stared at herself in the mirror. She blinked a few times.

I'd never seen Avery look this way before, with green paint or without.

She was beaming.

At me.

"Wren," she said. "Do you *know* you're a genius? *Do* you? Because you've totally turned me into Elphaba! Omigod, I love it! We *have* to go show Ms. Belfonte!"

Everyone went crazy over Avery's makeup, begging me to do theirs next. Ms. Belfonte had to explain that I wasn't doing everybody's makeup—the cast was too big, and we'd have parents helping backstage anyway. But perhaps I could assist with Madame Morrible and Dr. Dillamond . . . ?

By now I'd done enough video research to know these two characters: the evil headmistress and the talking-goat professor. And remembering what Poppy had told me— how I should know something about the show—I'd even watched a few of their scenes on YouTube.

Nothing boring-vanilla about their makeup, I had to admit. They could be fun, actually.

But to add them to Elphaba? To do *all three characters* right before the curtain? Could I even work that fast?

"Wren, you *have* to!" Avery shouted at me in her onstage-Elphaba voice. "This is not a choice!"

"Please?" Minna said, making begging hands.

"I guess I could try," I told Ms. Belfonte.

Poppy threw her arms around me, lifting me a foot off

the floor. It felt like a mile, and made me almost dizzy, but not in a bad way.

"Wren, I *knew* you could do it!" she shouted. "Didn't I *tell* you? Aren't you happy I made you?"

Over Poppy's shoulder I spotted Kai looking at me. Our eyes met; then he looked away.

"Yeah, I am," I admitted as my feet touched the floor again.

Poppy cupped her hand over my ear to whisper. "And? Have you changed your mind about Avery? She's not so bad, right?"

I thought about that. Avery was ecstatic with me because I'd transformed her into Elphaba. She wasn't suddenly my friend—but of course an ecstatic Avery was a good thing. Especially compared with a furious Annika.

And I was proud of myself for dealing with her. No, more than just "dealing": showing what I could do.

Something has changed within me. / Something is not the same. . . .

"I can handle Avery," I told Poppy, who smiled at me with shining eyes.

Baby Yoda

Two weeks later was our first dress rehearsal.

It wasn't a complete disaster, even though one of the horns I'd made for Dr. Dillamond kept falling off Mateo's head. Also: Gracie Ng blanked out on the lyrics halfway through "Popular," two flats wobbled, Emmett's voice cracked in "As Long As You're Mine," and one of the spotlights kept blinking until Kai did something to fix the light board.

"Kai to the rescue," Ms. Chen said, giving him a fist bump. Henry, Pippa, and Aliyah fist-bumped him too. Kai let our knuckles brush, dropped his eyes, and turned away.

Well, fine, I told myself. *Be like that.*

But really, I was more sad than mad. Because the way things had been going with Kai since Valentine's Day, no way could we ever be friends. Not if he wouldn't even look at me.

I told myself it shouldn't matter, but it did. Which was funny, in a way, because he was the one with no friends, and I had Poppy.

So the morning after dress rehearsal I walked over to him in math. "Hey, Kai, can I show you something?" I said, as if nothing bad-weird had ever happened, no one had given anyone a valentine, we'd been chatting like this every day.

He was so shocked he dropped his notebook.

As he bent to get it, I put my phone on his desk. "Check out this webcomic I found," I said. "It's called *My Six Legs*. Insect-themed, not in a *Wingz* sort of way, but I think you'll like it."

He frowned at my phone. For a second I thought he'd refuse to read it. But all of a sudden he started scrolling.

Then he looked up, right at me. "Not stupid," he said.

When I got home from school that day, Mom's car wasn't in the driveway. She hadn't left me a note, which was odd. And after being scolded by Krystal, I didn't want to call Mom at work, or even text, unless it was "important."

What time had Mom left for work today? Had she even walked Lulu before she left? Judging by how frantic Lulu was to get outside, it was possible she hadn't. I took Lulu up and down our block a few times, then fed her some kibble in the kitchen.

Once she'd settled herself on the sofa, I went upstairs to Mom's bedroom. Of course her door was shut. Of course it was locked.

"Mom? You in there?" I called. "Mom? Mom?"

I banged on the door, rattled the knob, but no answer. *Well, but she's been good lately,* I reminded myself. Working hard, keeping regular hours, mostly. She'd probably left for work this morning in a hurry; maybe there was an emergency in the ER. I shouldn't assume anything bad.

I went into my room and turned on my computer to study videos of Dr. Dillamond and Madame Morrible. And right away I stopped thinking about Mom because—great news! A new video from Cat FX! Her first in more than a month!

> *Hey, guys, Cat FX here. Sorry I haven't posted recently. I've been busy adulting and . . . you don't want to hear all that stuff, I'm guessing. So anyway, before we get started with Baby Yoda, I have some incredibly exciting news! I just found out I'm doing a makeup demo at the Chicago Comic Con! I know, right? My friend, the ah-may-zing makeup artist Tigr Lily, had to cancel, and I'm the replacement. So if you're in the Chicagoland area this Saturday, I hope I'll see you there! It's going to be the*

*greatest Comic Con of all time! Literally. Cannot.
Wait.*

*Okay, where were we? Baby Yoda! This one's
pretty advanced, you guys. But worth it, because
he's so stinkin' adorable, right? So let's get started.
First up we delete the eyebrows. . . .*

My brain exploded. *Cat FX was coming to Comic Con.*
The Comic Con that Kai had invited me to! And then
uninvited me, presumably. Although he'd never *said* I was
uninvited. And he'd read that webcomic on my phone, so
maybe he didn't hate me so much anymore. Although
even if he forgave me a teeny bit, it didn't mean he'd want
to spend an entire day with me, probably.

Could I go anyway? I checked the website. Tickets were
expensive, and of course my Chanuk-mas money was
gone. Also: Comic Con was happening *next weekend*. The
same weekend, same time, as *Wicked*! So that meant Kai
wasn't going either!

Crap. Crapcrapcrap.

Well, somehow I'd be there. I couldn't figure out how
to make that happen. But it *would* happen, I told myself.
Because it had to.

Chill

The thought of Cat FX coming to Comic Con set off fireworks in my brain. So I was wide-awake when Krystal called my phone at ten that night.

"Hey, honey," she said in her friendly-but-not-too-friendly voice. "Your mom there? I tried her cell, but she isn't answering."

I said she wasn't home. "Are you at the hospital? Isn't she there?"

"No, she's off today. You didn't know that?"

"Oh riiiight," I said. "I mean, I knew, but I forgot. Is everything okay?"

"Sure. We just need to discuss the schedule. I know she's off tomorrow, too, so I'll try to catch her in the morning." Krystal paused. "Everything's fine, honey. You should go to bed now, all right?"

"Yeah, I will," I said. "Bye."

But now I felt hot sweaty and cold sweaty. *If Mom isn't at work, where is she?*

I crawled under my covers with my phone. Sleep was impossible; I'd watch a Cat FX video, I told myself. Because even ones I'd already seen a hundred times were comforting. Evil Tooth Fairy. Deadpool. The mermaid . . .

So when the garage door grunched open sometime after midnight, I sprang out of bed to grab Mom's arm before she could lock her door on me.

"Where were you?" I demanded.

"What?" Her eyes were seeing me but not really *seeing* me.

It gave me a chill.

"Mom, you didn't leave me a note!" I said. "Did you forget? It's really late; I was worried. Are you okay?"

"I'm fine, Wren. Just tired. Long shift."

She was wearing yoga pants and a tee. Not scrubs.

"You were at the hospital?" My voice was shaky.

"Of course. Where else would I be?"

"I don't know." *Krystal said you were off today.* "Sometimes it's like you just disappear."

She groaned. "Okay, Wren, do we have to discuss all this right now? It's very late, and I need to sleep."

"Because you have work in the morning?"

She blinked. "Right, I do."

"But that's not true!"

"What?" Her leg wobbled; she grabbed the doorknob.

"Krystal called! She told me you *don't* have work tomorrow! So why are you saying that you *do*?"

All of a sudden I realized I didn't want to hear her answer, whatever it was.

I turned, went to my bedroom, and slammed my door.

Ticket

The next morning Mom was drinking coffee in her bathrobe when I came downstairs for breakfast. She seemed okay, rested. Her eyes were bright. Even her skin without the too-pink foundation was a decent color.

"Wren," she said, "I want to apologize about last night. I was talking to a doctor friend, it turned into dinner with a couple glasses of wine, and I guess we lost track of time. I'm so sorry if you were worried, and I promise I'll communicate better next time."

I peanut-buttered my bagel. So was Mom saying she'd had a *date* with this "doctor friend"? And also telling me she'd gotten drunk? It would definitely explain how out-of-it she'd seemed when she came home last night.

Maybe she was expecting me to ask for details. But I didn't have room in my head for this conversation, so

I basically pretended we weren't having it. "Today's the final dress rehearsal," I said. "We're doing the show twice, Friday night and Saturday matinee. Do you want a ticket?"

"You need to ask? Of *course* I want a ticket! You think your mom would miss your big makeup debut?" She laughed. "Krystal wants to come too. And bring Tucker. Can you get us three tickets for tomorrow night?"

"I'll try."

"Excellent! Oh, and I'll come to the Saturday matinee, too. I'll arrange my work schedule so I can."

I chewed my bagel. "You don't have to. The makeup will be exactly the same as Friday night."

"I know, but I'm just so proud of you, baby! Can't a mom celebrate her daughter's beautiful, brilliant work?"

"Yeah, okay," I said. "I mean, I'll *try* to get tickets for both performances. Will you be here after school today?"

"Why?" Mom seemed surprised by the question.

But I didn't want to have that conversation either.

"Just wondering," I said.

At lunch Poppy was so nervous about the final dress rehearsal after school that she couldn't stop talking. Even for her, she was loud and chattery; I tried to tune her out as I nibbled my turkey chili.

"Wren, you okay?" she asked after a few minutes. "You seem out of it."

"Sorry."

"Are you scared about the show? Don't be! Avery and Minna are totally in love with your makeup! And I know Mateo had some problems with his horns, but—"

"It's not about the show," I said quietly, glancing around the table to make sure no one was listening. "I'm just mad at my mom."

"You are?" She leaned toward me and dropped her voice. "Did you guys have a fight?"

"Not exactly." *I should tell her something, shouldn't I? Otherwise, what's the point of having a friend?* "It's hard to explain. Sometimes Mom is great, but sometimes it's like . . . she forgets I'm even there."

Poppy's eyes were big. "Oh, Wren. I'm sure she doesn't forget about you!"

"Maybe not *forget*. More like I go out of focus for her."

"Yeah? Well, you're lucky, then. I *wish* I went out of focus for my mom! You remember that math test when I got a sixty-eight? She totally freaked, and now I have to show her my math notebook every night. *Plus* she hired a math tutor." Poppy shuddered. "A mom who's not in your face every second sounds *awesome* to me, actually."

I shrugged. I knew Poppy was right; I'd go crazy if I had a parent who helicoptered all the time.

But I couldn't stop thinking about this other feeling I had: how sometimes when Mom looked at me, it was like she didn't even see my face. Like my features had been deleted, one by one, and all she was seeing when I stood in front of her was white foundation, and powder, layer on top of layer, making me go blurry.

Until finally I disappeared too.

Dress Rehearsal

The funny thing about Kai was that when we were backstage together, he talked to me all the time. Not in a friendly way, more in a "Can you please use that other table; we need this one for the props" sort of way. Exactly the same way he talked to Henry, Pippa, and Aliyah. Of course, I didn't expect us to be chatting about webcomics or superheroes—we were both working hard, focused on show things: him on the lights and sound effects, me on the makeup for three important characters.

Of the three, Madame Morrible was the easiest: I basically just needed Clown White, Rusty Nail eye shadow (which I also used for her cheeks), chocolate-brown eyebrow pencil, and Poison Apple lipstick. Minna stayed perfectly still while I worked, not fidgeting or chatting, and only when I finished did I realize she wasn't wearing her back brace.

It was funny to see tiny, whispery Minna morph into the evil schoolmistress. "Hey, nice, Wren," she said when she looked at herself in the mirror. "I look really scary, don't I?"

She sprang from her chair before I could even remove the towel around her neck.

Mateo was another story. The tricky thing about Dr. Dillamond, the goat/professor, was keeping his horns and ears on his head. For the first two dress rehearsals they'd kept breaking off, so Ms. Chen had glued them to a latex swim cap, which Mateo was supposed to wear.

But Mateo kept tugging on the cap, pulling it down over his left eye, so the horns and ears didn't line up in a row. Also, when I tried to paint on wrinkles, he kept twitching. And squinting. And talking. About some basketball game he went to, some TV series he was streaming, blahblah-blah.

"Mateo, *please* just try to zone out," I told him.

"Can't, I'm too nervous," he said. "And this stupid cap itches like crazy. Maybe I'm allergic?"

From a Cat FX video I knew there was such a thing as latex allergy. I peeked under the cap. But Mateo's brow looked normal, not pink or red or bumpy with hives.

"It looks fine," I told him. "Try to think about something else, okay? A calm place you like. Maybe the beach?"

So then he started blabbing about this lake his family went to last summer, how he went canoeing with his brother. I let him talk because it took his mind off the itchy swim cap. But all his talking made drawing wrinkles extremely tricky.

By this time Avery was used to the Elphaba makeup. She chatted (but not too much) while I layered the Landscape Green paint, and kept her mouth still when I did her lipstick. Were we friends? No, not even a little. But I wasn't scared of her anymore. And whenever I finished her makeup, she made a big deal of thanking me. So now I didn't even dread doing Elphaba.

For the final dress rehearsal, Kai stood nearby as I applied the finishing touches to Elphaba's mascara. The way he was watching made me jittery, and as soon as Avery ran off to show Ms. Belfonte, he came over.

"You've improved a lot, Wren," he said.

"Oh, you mean I used to be terrible?" I raised my eyebrows.

Maybe he didn't get that I was teasing. He frowned. "No, no. I just meant the first time you did Elphaba it was good, and now it's even better."

"Thanks," I said, smiling.

Was he blushing? I thought he might be. But he turned away too fast for me to be sure.

Commotion

Finally it was opening night. Mom had a day shift at the hospital on Friday. So she said she'd meet Krystal and Tucker in the lobby of the auditorium.

"Save us seats as close to the stage as possible," Mom told me at breakfast Friday morning.

"I'll try," I said. "But I'm sure a lot of parents will get there early. Poppy said her mom's reserving a whole row."

Mom's face clouded. "Wren, please don't guilt me because I have to work."

"I'm not guilting you! I'm just saying it just might be hard to save three good seats."

"Well, I'll get there as fast as I possibly can! You know how excited I am. How much I've been looking forward to tonight."

Suddenly I felt like the worst daughter in the world.

I got up from my chair to hug her. "Sorry, Mom," I said. "I didn't mean anything."

She kissed my hair, gulped down the rest of her coffee, and left for the hospital.

The teachers didn't even pretend it was a regular school day. They knew all the drama kids were super distracted, so for some classes we watched movies. For music we just all met in the auditorium, though considering how nervous everyone was, especially the leads, I wondered if that was a good idea.

"Omigod, what if I totally blank out and forget all my lines?" Avery was squealing.

"I'm sure that won't happen," Ms. Belfonte told her. "But just in case, I'll be right in the front to prompt you."

"What if my horns fall off again?" Mateo said. "Or my ears?"

"Then we'll glue them back on. People, try to relax—"

"What if the stage spontaneously combusts?" Emmett asked. "And the school gets hit by a giant meteorite? And it's the Ice Age all over again?"

"Not funny, Emmett," Poppy said. She swatted his arm.

I couldn't listen. Instead I watched Kai scurrying around, organizing the prop table for Aliyah, writing sticky notes on the dimmer board for Pippa and on the sound board for Henry. He seemed—not calm, exactly, but focused in a way that I envied.

If anyone messes up tonight, it won't be Kai, I thought.

Curtain was at seven, and with all the preshow preparation, most of us didn't bother going home after school. Poppy's mom ordered the cast ten pizzas for dinner, and Avery's mom brought trays of cupcakes with green frosting. Some kids (Poppy, for example) were so nervous they couldn't stop eating. Other kids (like me) were too nervous to even think about food.

At five fifteen I did Minna's makeup, at five thirty I did Mateo's, and at five forty-five I started Avery's. All my practice had paid off; by now I knew how long every step would take. Still, I kept checking the wall clock to make sure I was pacing myself, not spending too much time on any one effect.

"Wren, do I look scared?" Avery asked as I brushed on the last bit of Magic Mauve.

"Nah, you look like Elphaba," I told her. "Fierce."

"You really mean that?"

"Oh, definitely. What's that line Elphaba says about commotions?"

"'*I don't cause commotions; I am one.*'"

"Exactly," I said. "You look like a commotion."

"Thanks, Wren. Can I say something?"

"Sure."

Avery clutched my arm with damp, icy fingers. "Sorry if I was mean to you before, okay? It was just because I didn't know you very well. I thought you were weird, and you were always so judgy—"

I almost laughed. "*I* was judgy?"

"Yeah. The way you're always watching everybody and never talking—"

"I talk! I talk a lot! I'm just quiet sometimes."

"*And* Poppy wouldn't shut up about how cool you were. Plus I thought you liked Kai—"

I pulled my arm away. "What if I did?"

Avery's perfectly redefined eyebrows shot up. "*Do* you? Like Kai?"

"No, not like that! But I don't get why anyone even cares. Including you, Avery."

Avery twisted her lips and shrugged.

And that was when I noticed Kai standing behind her, listening to the whole conversation, probably.

I opened my mouth, but he walked away before any words came out.

Reserved

was right about one thing: Loads of parents started showing up at six, reserving all the best seats with coats, scarves, and backpacks. So I ripped three pages out of my math notebook, wrote *RESERVED FOR WREN LEWIS*, and left them on seats in the fourth row for Mom, Krystal, and Tucker.

For the next forty minutes, I watched from the wings as the auditorium filled with happy, noisy families. Dads taking photos of the set. Moms gabbing to other moms. Sisters and brothers and grandparents all buzzing. My three seats with the *RESERVED* signs still empty.

Would I be the only kid without a cheering section?

My stomach twisted. *Where is everybody?*

At 6:48, my phone buzzed. Krystal.

Outside auditorium now, you hear from your mom? she texted.

No, but she said she was meeting you in the lobby!! I texted back.

Guess she's running late. ☹ Where are seats?

Row 4. I put Reserved signs.

Ty, she replied.

"Ten minutes to curtain," Ms. Belfonte said. "Places, everyone."

"Omigod, I have to pee!" Gracie Ng shouted.

"Well, hurry!" Ms. Belfonte said.

I checked the audience again. Still no Mom.

Four minutes later Krystal came racing down the aisle, holding the hand of a little boy who was obviously Tucker. Apologizing as they made their way to the seats. Taking off their jackets. Sitting.

Without Mom.

6:55. 6:56.

My heart hammered.

"You okay, Wren?" Poppy murmured in my ear.

"Yeah," I said. "My mom's not here, though."

"Maybe she's stuck in traffic. I'm sure she'll make it in time. Want some water? You look a little funny."

"No thanks, I'm fine. You should take your place now."

Poppy squeezed my arm and ran off.

Did Mom disappear on me again?

The curtain opened and the show began.

Nurse Mode

The show went great. At least, that was how it seemed, based on the standing ovation from the audience, and the way everyone in the cast hugged each other when it was over, laughing and crying and smearing all their makeup.

I mean, yes, I was there the whole time, watching the whole thing from the wings. Listening to all the music. *No one mourns the wicked. Pop-u-lar like me. De-fy-ing graaaaav-ity. Because I knew you, I have been changed for good.* But it was like I was hearing the music underwater, or watching a movie through a streaky window. All of it seemed loud and emotional and very far away.

Plus all that love-duet stuff was incredibly embarrass-ing, really. Who'd decided that this was what love looked like—people waving their arms around while they held long notes and spat into each other's faces? I didn't have a crush on anyone—but if I did, I couldn't imagine it making me behave that way. Super exaggerated and so . . . fake.

The one thing that seemed real to me was the empty seat in the auditorium. The *only* empty seat. Which stayed empty, even though Krystal tried calling Mom three times during intermission, and I texted her in caps: WHERE ARE YOU? and MOM, WHAT'S GOING ON?

"Must be an emergency at the hospital," Krystal told me as she and Tucker took their seats right before the start of Act Two.

"Wouldn't she tell us if there was?" I asked.

"Come on, Wren, you know how it is. When things get rough in the ER, nurses can't stop to make outside calls. And I told you how our supervisor feels about your mom on the phone so much."

Well, true. Hearing that calmed me for maybe three minutes. But by the end of Act Two, when Elphaba takes off with Fiyero, I felt cold sweaty. Like my head was carbonated and I couldn't breathe.

So the second everyone finished taking their bows, I ran over to Krystal. "I need to get out of here," I said.

Right away she went into ER-nurse mode. "Let's get you home," she said crisply, pulling me past the proud parents and gushing grandmas who blocked the aisles.

Outside the building I gulped some air while Krystal and Tucker found their car. Krystal didn't say a word as she pulled up to the curb and opened the passenger door.

"Are you sick?" Tucker asked from the back seat. "You gonna throw up in our car?"

I shook my head as I buckled the seat belt.

Krystal glanced at Tucker. "Wren is okay, buddy. Just a little upset."

"Why is she just a little upset?" Tucker asked.

"She's worried about her mom, but I'm sure everything's fine. Did you like the show, buddy?"

"I liked the quiet parts."

"I know what you mean," I told him, looking out the window.

Krystal patted my hand. "Well, Wren, I thought your makeup was beautiful. And don't worry, I took plenty of photos."

Ugh. I'd promised Dad makeup pictures, but with all the where's-Mom business, I'd completely forgotten. Well, I'd have another chance to take photos at the matinee tomorrow.

Krystal put on the radio so at least we didn't have to talk until we pulled up to our street about three minutes later.

And saw Mom's car parked in the driveway. The kitchen light on inside our house.

For a second I sat in Krystal's passenger seat, frozen.

Mom is home? All this time?

"Wren, you want us to come inside with you?" Krystal asked gently. A voice that wasn't her bossy-nurse voice.

"No, it's okay." I unbuckled the seat belt. "But thanks for the ride."

"Of course," Krystal said. "And, Wren?"

I looked at her.

"You did really great tonight, honey. I'm proud of you."

"Thank you."

Blinking away tears, I ran inside the house.

Math Problem

I ran past Lulu's slobbery, frantic greeting, straight into the living room, where Mom was sprawled on the sofa, dressed in her scrubs. Snoring.

"Mom!" I shouted. I pushed her shoulder. "Wake up!"

Her face scrunched in her sleep like she was solving a complicated math problem.

I pushed harder. "Mom! Get up—you missed my show!"

At last she stirred. "Wait, what?"

"Mom, you missed *Wicked* tonight! I saved you a seat and you never came! Krystal and Tucker were there, but I was the only kid without a parent! What happened to you?"

"Oh no. Oh, Wren, I'm so sorry." Slowly, she sat up. Her voice dragged and her eyes looked heavy, like Person with a

Bad Cold. "I haven't been sleeping lately, and it was a busy shift, so when I got home, I thought I'd take a quick nap—"

"I don't care!" By now I'd given up fighting back tears. They splashed all over my face like a hot summer rainstorm. "You always have some excuse, and I don't want to hear it, okay?"

"Wren, sweetheart, please—"

"And you know what? I'm sorry I told Dad and Vanessa not to come! They wanted to, but I said no, because I thought *you'd* be upset. I always think about *your* feelings, but you never think about *mine*!"

"Wren, you know that's not true—"

"Poppy's mom works as hard as you do, and she was there! She was even *early*. And she helped with the makeup and brought us all pizza!"

Why was I even saying this? I didn't care about the pizza. Or about Poppy's mom.

"Oh, honeybee," Mom said. "I don't know what to say except I'm sorry. But I'll definitely be there tomorrow for the matinee, okay? You know I purposely arranged my schedule—"

All of a sudden I had the underwater feeling again, like all her words were whooshing in the ocean, echoing from somewhere miles off. Like she was talking, making human sounds, but I couldn't even tell in what language.

"I'm going to bed now," I announced before she could say anything else. "Good night!"

I ran upstairs and watched Cat FX—so close that very weekend, just at Comic Con in downtown Chicago, but also so far away.

The Sign

For the Saturday matinee Ms. Belfonte told us to be at school by noon. I woke up at nine, splashed some freezing-cold water on my face, got dressed, and took Lulu out for a walk.

By the time we came back, I realized that my head was throbbing and my stomach felt hollow.

Had I caught one of Mom's hospital bugs? Probably I was just hungry, considering that last night I'd been too upset to eat any supper.

I made myself a bagel-and-peanut-butter sandwich. Then I washed the dishes (including the ones from yesterday) and emptied the stinky trash.

At 11:20 Mom's door was still shut. And of course locked. I tried calling her through the door. No answer.

Here we go again, I thought. *Well, either she set her alarm*

or she didn't. I can't wait around for her to wake up. If she doesn't care about my show, fine!

I packed some extra supplies in my backpack—Magic Mauve, Clown White, Magenta Magic, a few of Vanessa's fancy brushes—and walked the six blocks to school.

Poppy ran over as soon as I entered the auditorium. "Wren, where did you go last night? I looked for you after the show, but you disappeared!"

Mom disappears, not me. "My mom's friend had to leave," I said.

She lowered her voice. "So . . . what happened to your mom?"

"She fell asleep on the sofa." I shrugged. "She says she's coming today. But who knows."

"Oh, okay." Poppy's warm brown eyes were full of sympathy, plus something else that I realized was confusion. Because, yes, I'd told her I'd been mad at Mom lately—but even so, sleeping through your kid's show was definitely something Poppy couldn't imagine.

"Anyhow, Wren, your makeup was amazing last night," she said. "All the parents said! And Ms. Belfonte told everyone that one day you'll be a famous makeup artist."

"She said that? Whoa." I smiled for the first time since yesterday.

And maybe because Poppy's words made me feel a little better, I picked up a playbill somebody had tossed in the aisle, wrote *RESERVED FOR KELLY LEWIS*, and stuck it on a seat in the second row.

Everything that happened afterward was because of that *RESERVED* sign.

Escape

Hey, guys, it's me, Cat FX.

So before we get to today's character, I want to share something I've been thinking about a lot lately. I know I'm always telling you to follow my instructions—do these steps in this order, right? And you really should, especially if you're just starting out with special-effects makeup.

But after a while, if you're serious about this stuff, you need to improvise. Because—trust me here, guys—doing special-effects makeup is not just about imitating me, or any other artist. You need to figure out your own characters and develop your own techniques.

Oh, and this is really important: never be afraid to take some risks!

∘ ○ ∘

I started the makeup at twelve thirty: first Madame Morrible, then Dr. Dillamond, then Elphaba. By now I didn't even have to think as I applied powder, foundation, pigment, lines, shadows. I could chat without thinking too. *Last night was great, Minna. You did great, Mateo. What a great audience.*

Avery acted like she completely forgot what she'd said to me last night, and I let her. Because as she fidgeted and squirmed while I transformed her into Elphaba, I realized I didn't even care anymore. She was just a bunch of facial features to color in Landscape Green. To contour and redefine. And when I finished my work, I could walk away, focus on more important things.

Specifically this: with twelve minutes until curtain, the seat I'd reserved for Mom was still empty.

And this: somewhere in downtown Chicago, Cat FX was appearing at Comic Con.

These two thoughts had nothing to do with each other, but also everything. All I wanted was for Mom to see my makeup. But if she wasn't coming—*again*—why was I even here, watching my classmates sing sappy love duets? When I could be somewhere that really mattered?

"Ten minutes to curtain," Ms. Belfonte called out. "Places, everyone."

Across the stage Poppy gave me a sympathy smile. I nodded and gave her a thumbs-up.

One last peek into the audience before the lights dimmed.

One empty seat, second row center.

A sign that said *RESERVED.*

But for who? For what?

Right at that moment I knew only one thing: I couldn't just stay here, staring into the auditorium, sweating and barely breathing, hoping that any second Mom would come running down the aisle, find the *RESERVED* sign, take her seat, remove her jacket, smile at the other parents. Blow me a kiss, take a photo. Because obviously none of this would ever happen.

And I can't even say I wondered what to do next. It was like my brain had stopped working, and something else was taking over. The sort of instinct that tells an animal there's fire nearby.

Escape. Now.

I ran over to Kai, who was standing by the prop table, checking for the zillionth time that all the props were there, in order, ready for Aliyah to hand to the actors.

"Can I please talk to you, Kai?" I begged. "Somewhere private?"

He blinked. "Can't it wait? The show's about to start."

"Yeah, I realize that. Please!"

I think he saw something desperate in my eyes, because he scowled, told Aliyah something about Glinda's wand, and led me over to the janitor's closet.

"Okay, talk fast," he said as Pippa dimmed the lights and the opening notes of "No One Mourns the Wicked" filled the auditorium.

I took a breath. "Kai, I really think we should go to Comic Con."

"What? You mean tomorrow?" He practically shouted it. "What are you talking about, Wren? I didn't think you even wanted to go."

"Shhh," I said. "No, no, I really do! And it has to be today, because Cat FX will be there—"

"*Who?*"

"That makeup artist I told you about! The one who does videos, remember? And you said you had tickets—"

"Yeah, my dad got them months ago. But—"

"They don't need us here! I finished the cast makeup, Aliyah's fine with props, and Pippa and Henry are doing lights and sound!"

Kai shook his head.

"Why are you shaking your head?" My voice squeaked.

"A million reasons. First of all, what if something went wrong with the dimmer board?"

"Ms. Chen would fix it! Or Pippa, or someone else! You're not the only one who—"

"And second, how would we get there?"

"Isn't your dad here? In the audience?"

"He came last night. Right now he's at the gym. So he can't drive us."

Ugh. I hadn't thought about transportation. I hadn't thought about any details, really.

"Fine, so we'll take the train into the city," I said. "You still have the tickets, right?"

"Yeah, on my phone," Kai admitted. He shoved his hands in his pockets and looked at the floor. "But, Wren, I heard what you told Avery yesterday, all right? How you don't even like me."

My face burned. "No, no! I *do* like you! As a friend! That's what I was trying to tell you when you gave me that valentine."

"It wasn't a valentine."

"Whatever it was! Kai, listen: I really want us to be friends! I want to hang out and talk about comics! And art! And cosplay! Even if we don't go to Comic Con."

He raised his eyebrows. "You mean that?"

"Yeah," I said. Then the words tumbled out of me. "Because we like the same sort of stuff, right? That's why I showed you that webcomic, *My Six Legs*. I didn't show it to anyone else, not even Poppy. To be honest, I don't think she'd get it."

He didn't say anything. But I could tell he was listening.

"Anyhow, if we *did* go to Comic Con, I could do your makeup," I added quickly.

"I guess," he said. "But I dunno. Running away without telling anyone?"

"We're not 'running away'! We're doing this one cool thing. For one afternoon!"

He shrugged.

Now the music onstage reached my ears. *And like every family, they had their secrets . . .*

"Listen, Kai, I really need to see Cat FX, so I'm going even if you don't," I said. "I'd rather go with you, because it'll definitely be more fun, and I won't be mad if you say no, okay? We're friends either way, I promise. But I'm leaving, so you need to decide right now."

"But you don't have a ticket." That was when a shy smile inched across his face. "Could you do Thanos? I know I told you I was thinking about Daredevil, but I changed my mind."

"I could do anyone you want," I said. "I'm sure of it."

I was so excited right then, it wasn't even a lie.

Thanos

You know how in some dreams everything happens in slow motion? The next part was like a dream that happened fast.

I ran back to the makeup table, grabbed my jacket, and tossed a bunch of supplies in my backpack. Then Kai led us out a backstage door I didn't even know existed.

The train station was ten blocks from school. Kai said he knew that there was a 1:47 train into the city on Saturdays, because he and his dad took it often—to go to museums, the aquarium, concerts, shows.

"Wow," I said as we walked fast in the chilly air. "My mom never takes me anywhere."

"How come?"

Too busy disappearing. "Working," I said.

We got to the station just before the train arrived—

barely enough time to get round-trip tickets from the ticket machine. Kai punched in the numbers as if he'd done this a million times before.

When the train doors opened, we took two opposite seats: Kai facing backward, me facing forward.

We're actually doing this, I thought. I grinned at Kai, but he didn't grin back.

"You okay?" I asked.

"Yeah," he said. "Just feeling a little . . . guilty."

"For what? Leaving the show?"

He shook his head. "Stealing the tickets. From my dad."

"But you didn't steal anything! Your dad *bought* the tickets, right? And you said he got an extra one for you to share with a friend. So I'm sure he'll be happy." I knew this was pushing it; I changed the subject fast. "Anyhow, let's get started on the makeup. Can you get a picture of Thanos on your phone?"

Kai did, just as the conductor came by to see our tickets and then chat for a bit (although I could tell he was mostly snooping about why two kids were heading into the city without a grown-up).

When the conductor finally quit asking his cheery, snoopy questions, I studied the Thanos picture and got to work. Foundation, Clown White, black kohl for lines in his chin: nothing too complicated, but it would be tricky to apply all the stuff on a vibrating train. And did I have the right shade of purple? Maybe not, but Je T'aime Amethyst was close enough. Fortunately, I'd grabbed one of Mateo's spare swim caps, so at least Thanos could have a bald head.

When I thought we had a good-enough Thanos, I put my phone in selfie and showed Kai.

"Hey, cool," he said, smiling for the first time since we left school.

Then I did Nebula for myself: not my best work, but not terrible, either, considering the moving train, the staring passengers, my sweaty hands.

"Okay, now we both turn off our phones," I said as over the PA a robot voice announced that our stop was next.

"Wait, really? What for?" Kai frowned.

"We're in character, right? We can't be distracted; we have to fully commit."

I knew it sounded as if I was quoting someone. Did Cat FX ever talk about "fully committing"? Probably yes, although I couldn't remember when.

But the real reason I'd said it was this: if Kai texted his dad, I knew he'd come to get us right away—and the two of us needed to be unrescuable.

Emerald City

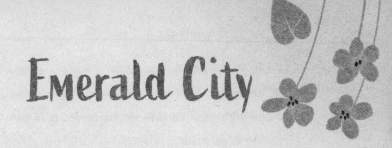

The train station was connected to the convention center, so when we arrived, we didn't even have to go outdoors. As we speed-walked through the tunnel, Kai seemed even more nervous than he was on the train.

"Doors close at six," he muttered. "And they kick you out at seven. So we need to hurry."

"We're hurrying," I said. "And don't use your hand to wipe your nose; you'll smear everything. Here." I gave him a crumpled old tissue from my jacket pocket. "Blot gently."

Kai took the tissue and blotted.

"You look great," I told him. He did a wince-smile.

As soon as we got to the main entrance, though, my heart sank. Because right under the neon WELCOME TO COMIC CON sign was another:

*All backpacks will be searched. No guns, weap-
ons, umbrellas, food allowed. All attendees under
the age of thirteen must be accompanied by a parent or legal guardian.*

Crap. How were we supposed to know that? Because I
hadn't seen that rule on the website.

"Okay, well, we tried," Kai said. His eyes darted like he
was ready to flee.

"Are you serious?" I said. "We're not just turning
around after all this!"

"Well, what are we supposed to do, then? Grab some
random grown-up off the street?"

I made a *shh* finger and pointed to a group of about thirty
kids and grown-ups—most of them cosplaying Avengers,
others doing *Toy Story* or *Frozen* or *Moana.* Laughing and
shouting and shoving as they opened their backpacks for
the guards, who waved metal detectors like high-tech ver-
sions of Glinda's wand.

"Come on." I grabbed Kai's sleeve and pulled him so
that we blended in with the big, noisy group.

And it worked. The guards were so busy checking bags
and tickets that they didn't stop us, or ask a bunch of
snoopy questions like the train conductor had.

We were in!

"Cool," Kai said as we raced into the convention hall.

As for me, I couldn't even talk. It was like we'd entered some portal and were now in another dimension—an Emerald City of pulsing lights and roaring music. Crowds of people in full costume pushed past us, heading for panels and demonstrations and cosplay competitions, posing for selfies with stuff they'd bought ("merch," Kai called it) like posters and inflatable Jedi swords, eating churros and blue slushies like they were at a baseball game or something.

It was all deafening and blinding, exactly what I needed. But where was Cat FX? How would I find her in all this . . . the best word was "commotion"?

Kai seemed to read my mind. He handed me a flyer that he'd picked up at the entrance.

"We could just walk around," he said. "But since we're watching the clock, I suggest we check out the schedule and see if there's anything we don't want to miss."

You may be watching the clock, but not me, I thought. *This is where I live now, Kai.*

But I knew he was right. And when I scanned the schedule, I saw that at five thirty—forty-seven minutes from now!—Cat FX was doing a demo called Special-Effects Makeup 101.

We weren't too late! She was here! I'd get to see her! In person!

"You okay, Wren?" Kai asked. He looked worried. Or, rather, Thanos did.

"I'm great!" I shouted above the *Star Wars* music that was blaring in front of a booth called TROOPER PRODUCTS: FASHION ACCESSORIES AND COLLECT-IBLES. "I'm just really excited about this one makeup demo, but it's not for a while! You want to see this panel first—Navigating the *Star Wars* Universe?" I pointed to a small stage where three guys were in folding chairs. Behind them was a screen showing a chart so complicated it was like peeking inside the human brain.

"Nah," Kai said. "Let's check out the one on Spider-Man storyboards. It's this way."

I let Kai lead us through the hall. To be honest, I didn't care what panel we were heading for. Only minutes to go until Cat FX! Who was inside this building! Breathing this same french-fries-scented air!

All my bones vibrated to the music.

When the storyboard panel was over, Kai asked one of the artists to sign a small sketchbook he kept in the pocket of his jacket. But first he showed the guy his drawings of Daredevil and Iceman, and the guy told him he was "super talented," that he should keep at it, and one day, who knows? Maybe Kai could be up on the stage beside him.

"Can you believe it?" Kai yelled at me. "Did you hear what he said?"

"Yes, I did." I grinned. "Aren't you glad we came? Wasn't it worth it?"

"Yeah," Kai admitted. "When's that makeup thing?"

"Now, but you don't have to come. I mean, if there's something else you'd rather do—"

"That's okay. You came to my panel, so I'll come to yours."

When he said this, I had a strange reaction. A tiny part of me wanted to be here all by myself. Floating undetected through the hall like my mental mermaid, picking up souvenirs for camouflage, unattached to anyone or anything back home.

But most of me was just relieved. Because if Kai and I got separated, we might never find each other again in this huge, crowded place, and that would be scary.

And the truth was, this whole thing was way more fun with a friend.

Blue Violet

At five thirty, in Conference Room 15678B, Cat FX was taking products out of her makeup kit and arranging them, one by one, on a small table. Like maybe she was killing time, waiting for more people to show up.

Because the audience was only six people. Six including Kai and me.

I couldn't believe it. Where was everyone? Didn't they realize that a brilliant artist was here *in person*, sharing her precious secrets with the world?

Cat FX was tinier than I'd figured she'd be, wearing a Harley Quinn wig (mostly white, with two messy pigtails, one tinted red, one blue). Her eyes were outlined in kohl black, she had a small black heart on her left cheek, and her lips were cherry red, smudged in a way that you could tell was on purpose. A creepy character, one I hadn't seen her do before—but her voice was so familiar, it was like hearing someone speak my private thoughts.

"Well, I guess we should get started," she was saying. "Today I'd like to show you how to do Shuri from *Black Panther*, and I need a volunteer. Anyone?" She smiled—a little nervously, I thought.

Kai poked me. "You."

I almost raised my hand. But no. Much better to sit in the front row, watching her technique up close. Even though I'd seen her Shuri video at least fifteen times and had to stop my mouth from moving as she spoke.

Anyway, she picked some mom-aged woman sitting behind me.

When she finished the demo, the four other people in the audience, including the volunteer, stayed to chat with her for a minute. The volunteer gave her a hug and asked if they could do a selfie together. Cat FX said, "You bet," and the two of them posed in a way that was a teeny bit embarrassing—hands on hips and duck lips.

Then Cat FX laughed her familiar laugh, and I felt better.

Kai poked my elbow. "All right, what's next?"

"Um, I think I'd like to stay for a minute? To talk to her," I said.

"Cool, but I'm starving. Okay with you if I get some food and meet you back here in like fifteen minutes?"

I nodded.

"You want anything? Fries or pizza or a Coke . . . ?"

"No thanks." I hadn't eaten anything since the breakfast bagel, but the thought of food right now was impossible.

Kai left. I walked over to Cat FX, who was carefully putting away her supplies.

"Hi," I said.

She looked up and smiled. "Hey. Nice Nebula."

For a second, I'd forgotten my face was blue. "Oh! Thanks! I got it from your video."

"Really? That's awesome. And your boyfriend is Thanos, right?"

"He's not my boyfriend! Why does everyone *assume* that?"

Cat FX's fake eyelashes fluttered. She seemed surprised by my reaction—and I was horrified. Why did it matter what she thought about Kai and me? How could I snap like that at my idol?

"Sorry," I said in a croaky voice. "I didn't mean . . ." I was too embarrassed to even finish the sentence.

"Hey, no worries," she said calmly. "I totally get it—I'm not anybody's anything either. To be honest, I've got enough going on just being me." She shrugged, grinning. "And that changes every day! Some days I'm a scorpion; some days I'm a butterfly. Or Nebula. What's your name?"

"Wren, like the bird. It used to be Renata, but I changed it."

"Same. I was born Catherine Fox, but of course I was *destined* to be Cat FX. So, Wren-like-the-bird, can I show you something cool to do with that eye?"

I decided to be brave. "Could you show me the mermaid makeup instead? How you make it seem like you're seeing it underwater? And the light is always changing?"

She raised a redefined eyebrow. "You couldn't tell from the video?"

"No, and I looked like a thousand times. You say to use Seafoam Blue by CozMeticks, but it's semitranslucent, not iridescent. And too green."

"Yeah, that's right. Good catch." She tossed her Harley Quinn pigtails and laughed. "But it's just my little trade secret, so don't tell anyone, okay, Wren? This is between you and me."

I sat in the volunteer's chair. Cat FX dabbed some makeup remover on my left cheekbone and began applying the mermaid makeup, explaining how she achieved the special iridescent effect with a final layer of shimmery color called Blue Violet by MakeDown MakeUp.

The whole time she was working, I thought: *Why would anyone do a how-to video but still keep something secret?* It seemed almost . . . unfair.

I was about to ask that question. Then I thought: *Yeah, but everyone has secrets sometimes. And anyhow, she's not keeping it secret from ME.*

Not knowing what else to say (*This is great, I think you're great*), I pointed out that there was no such thing as a blue violet.

"Actually, blue violets *do* exist in nature," Cat FX said cheerfully. "Purple ones are more common, but just because something is weird doesn't mean it's not real." She squinted at my face, then reached into her makeup kit for a tiny brush. "And you know, Wren, blue is my *absolute favorite* color to work with, because it's so many things—the ocean and the sky. Cold, peace, and sadness. The god Krishna. Nebula, the X-Man Nocturne. Smurfs . . ."

As Cat FX went on and on about the color blue, I was happier than I'd ever been in my whole life. Sitting in that chair, talking about the thing I loved with the person I worshipped. *This is where I belong,* I told myself. *Not pulled in different directions. Being the true Wren.* Even though that meant wearing mermaid makeup. Blue Violet, which was secret and good weird. Beautiful and real.

All of a sudden Kai was standing in front of us. He was holding a blue slushy in one hand and his phone in the other. His eyes looked huge.

"Wren, we have to leave," he said. His voice sounded funny.

"Now?" I stared at him. "But we're not finished—"

"My dad's been texting. He knows where we are and he's really mad. He told me to ask for your mom's phone number."

My mom? "Kai, I thought you turned off your phone—"

"I did, but I turned it back on. You should turn on yours, too, maybe."

"Go ahead, Wren," Cat FX said gently. "Don't get in trouble because of me."

I took my phone out of my backpack and turned it on.

Nothing from Mom.

Three Where are you? messages from Poppy.

And from Krystal: Wren, something happened. Wherever you are, you need to get home now. Waiting here for you.

And: Why aren't you answering?

And then: Wren honey, your mom has just been admitted to the hospital. Pls pls hurry home.

The Hard Part

I can barely remember anything that happened right after that—how Kai and I raced out of the convention center. How we got on the next train to Donwood. How we rode home, still wearing our makeup. Not talking, Kai texting his dad.

Again we'd taken two opposite seats, and this time I was the one facing backward. The whole ride home I stared out the window, watching bright city lights streak by, blurring into other lights that were dimmer and farther apart. It felt like we were moving backward in time, even though I knew that was impossible. You couldn't undo anything that happened, no matter how hard you wished you could.

After the conductor (a grumpy woman) took our tickets without asking questions, Kai offered me half of a giant chocolate chip cookie he'd bought at the convention center.

I just shook my head. I couldn't even form the word "no."

But when the PA announcer called, "Donwood, next stop," I looked right at him. "Kai, I'm really sorry if I got you in trouble—"

"Don't be," he said. "I got myself in trouble."

"You're not mad?"

"At you? Nah." His brow furrowed. "It was my decision. I just hope your mom's okay."

I nodded, because already I'd run out of words.

Kai's dad was waiting for us in his car as we got off the train in Donwood. I guessed that Kai had been texting the news about Mom, because his dad didn't ask questions or scold us. And when he drove up to my driveway, he said that he hoped Mom would be okay, and that if I needed anything, I shouldn't hesitate to call. So I thought Kai's dad was nice, even if he'd probably start yelling at Kai the second I got out of the car.

My hands were shaking as I put the key in the front door. On the train I'd texted Krystal, so I knew she was waiting for me at home. And, of course I told her where I'd been, that I was okay and on the way back to Donwood. But I knew she wouldn't be happy to see me.

"Wren, is that you?" Immediately Krystal came running to the kitchen door, waving her arms, shouting. "How could you run off like that? What were you thinking? Going to the city all by yourself? Without telling anyone?"

"I wasn't by myself; I was with my friend Kai. And who cares about me! What's wrong with Mom?"

"Let's sit," Krystal said.

I followed her into the table without even taking off my jacket.

We took chairs facing each other. She grabbed a tissue from her pocket and wiped her nose.

"Wren," she said in a quiet voice that was scarier than her shouting voice, "I'm going to tell you something that'll be hard to hear. First I need to say that your mom is getting care by the best doctors at our hospital, and they say she's going to be okay. You hear me? *She'll be okay.* I want to hear you say that now."

I nodded, because you didn't disobey Krystal. "She'll be okay."

"All right, good. So here's the hard part, honey. What happened was that your mom overdosed on some pills she's been taking."

"She . . . what?"

"Yeah. I had a feeling that something was going on, some reason she never made it to your show last night, so I swung by this afternoon just to check in with her, you know? The front door wasn't locked, so I went in. And when I found her on the sofa, I did what I could, and then I called 911." Krystal took a new tissue. "Apparently she's been abusing these pills—painkillers—for quite a while now. Did you have any idea?"

Did I?

No. Of course not.

I shook my head. "I knew her knee hurt. And her back," I said. "But she's been saying that for a long time."

"Right. But nothing different about her behavior *lately*?"

No.

But also . . . maybe yes.

I opened my mouth to speak. Except no words came out. Only sobs.

Because a hundred things avalanched in my head right then: The disappearances. The locked door. All those unlabeled pills in her medicine cabinet. The way she freaked about me snooping in her bathroom. The stomach bugs. The phone calls at work that she blamed on me. The missing money. That empty look in her eyes, how she'd seemed drunk after that night with her "doctor friend" . . .

"But I thought she was a good nurse," I said, shudder-
ing as Krystal wrapped her arms around me and kissed my
sweaty hair. "You kept saying she was."

"Because it's true," Krystal said.

"So when she acted funny, I thought: okay, well, she
works so hard at the hospital, she has crazy hours, she
isn't sleeping well at night, it makes sense she's so out of it
when she gets home—"

"And all that's right."

"But the whole time at work . . . she was taking *pills*?"

Krystal pulled away to wipe her face. "This is the part
I don't completely understand either, honey. When your
mom was at the hospital, she was totally on her game."
She paused. "But every now and then, especially these last
couple of months, I guess, she did seem a little . . . off. Like
I told you how she kept disappearing on the floor, how our
supervisor would get mad. But Kelly would say she was
just talking to you on the phone—"

"Yeah, well. She wasn't."

"I'm sorry I scolded you about that, Wren. There's a lot
I got wrong. I keep going over it all in my mind, little things
that make sense to me now." Krystal shook her head. "Your
mom kept coming to work late these past few weeks, saying
it was a car problem, but she never took the car to the garage
to be checked out. So I figured it was a money thing. And

one time I walked into the nurses' bathroom, and I thought I saw something funny, so I asked her about it. But she denied it, she got upset at me, and I guess I just really wanted to believe her. And now I blame myself, because I'm a health professional; I'm supposed to know what I'm seeing. . . ."

It was Krystal's turn to cry. She didn't ugly-cry like me, though; she just sniffed and dabbed the corners of her eyes with a crumpled tissue.

"It's not your fault," I told her. "Mom is really good at hiding things. Can I ask you a question?"

"Of course."

"Was she with you on Christmas? With your whole family, I mean."

"Well, I invited her, because you were going to your dad's. But she said she didn't celebrate, so I didn't push it." Krystal sighed. "I guess your dad doesn't know any of this, right?"

"She doesn't like it if I talk to him about her. She calls it going behind her back."

"Yeah. That sounds like Kelly. Well, you know, we really shouldn't keep this from him. He needs to know."

I didn't argue. The separate makeup boxes had never worked, anyway.

All this time, I told myself, *Mom had a serious problem—a drug problem—and I saw everything, all the signs. But I just sort of stuffed them in a shoebox and shoved them under my bed. Pretended they weren't real. Obsessed about other things instead. Mermaid blue. Cat FX. Kai's valentine. Avery and Poppy. The show. Comic Con.*

I was the worst daughter in the world, wasn't I?

"I'm the worst daughter in the world," I said.

"Oh, Wren," Krystal said. "Of course you're not."

"But I saw the pills! I even asked why she had so many, and she said she had a knee doctor. At the hospital."

"And you believed her, because she's your mom. I know, honey, I know. But the knee pain is real; I'm sure about *that* much." Krystal reached across the table to take my hand. But not a hand sandwich—just holding my sweaty hand in her soft, warm palm.

Until I reached for a tissue to blow my nose. As I did, some Blue Violet came off on the tissue, making it seem like the whole Comic Con thing was a dream I was waking from. And this conversation was real life.

"So what's going to happen now?" I finally asked.

Krystal took a long, slow breath. "Your mom will be in detox at the hospital for four or five days. After that she'll go to a twenty-one-day program at an inpatient facility."

"Impatient?"

She smiled weakly. "*In*patient. That means she'll be staying there."

I almost asked, *What about me? Where will I go if Mom isn't here all that time?* Almost a whole month, if you added five pus twenty-one.

But it seemed like such a small detail to worry about, compared to everything else.

First Flight Out

That night Krystal insisted on staying over, even though I told her it wasn't necessary; I was used to taking care of myself. "Not a choice," she said, using her bossy-nurse voice again, so I didn't argue.

She went back to her house to get Tucker, who'd been watched by Tyndall. When they returned about an hour later, she was carrying a casserole dish of chili, a Tupperware of salad, and a tin of brownies. I could barely wait to set the table before stuffing my face with her amazing food. I hadn't eaten anything since the breakfast bagel, plus all the crying had added to my appetite.

By the time we finished washing the dishes, it was almost nine. But since tomorrow was Sunday, Krystal said Tucker could watch TV with us for a little while. So we put on *Toy Story 4*—and after about twenty minutes, both Tucker and Krystal were asleep on the sofa. I got them blankets from the linen closet and went upstairs to bed, not even watching any Cat FX videos before I fell fast asleep.

At ten fifteen the next morning, Krystal and Tucker were gone, and Dad was in the kitchen, drinking coffee from Mom's red mug.

He got up right away to hug me.

I went limp in his arms. "Why are you here?"

"*Why?* What kind of a question is that?"

"I mean, you know about Mom? Who told you?"

"Krystal called me late last night, so I got on the first flight out of JFK this morning. Does that surprise you?" He seemed annoyed. "You think I *wouldn't* be here for you, Wren? And for Mom, too?"

"Dad, please don't be mad."

"I'm not mad, sweetheart. I'm just . . ." He shook his head. "I'm really just upset at myself. Because I knew she was moody, I expected that, but when she stopped answering my calls, I should have pushed harder, asked more questions, I don't know . . ." His voice trailed off.

"But I didn't know about it either," I told him. "I mean, it was like I knew but I also didn't. A lot of the time Mom seemed fine." I took a breath. "And when she wasn't fine,

I wanted to tell you, but she was always mad at you. So I thought if I told you things, she'd just get mad at *me*."

"Yeah, I get that. It wasn't fair for you to be in the middle. And no one's blaming you, jellybean; none of this is your fault, okay? *None* of it." He kissed the top of my bedhead. "Anyhow, I'm here now."

"But what about Vanessa and the babies?"

"Vanessa understands that you have school here, and a busy social life, right? We both just want to do what's best for you while Mom is getting help. And if this means me hanging out in beautiful Donwood, working from my computer, that's what I'll do. Grandma Ellen will help Vanessa, and so will her other relatives. And of course we can Skype and FaceTime."

My brain couldn't process all this. "So you're just . . . going to stay with me? Here? While Vanessa stays in Brooklyn?"

"It's just for now," Dad said, nodding. "Let's take this one step at a time, okay?"

"Krystal said it could be a month."

"We'll figure it out, Wren." He wrapped his arms around me a second time.

And right at that moment I thought: *Well, of course he's here. He's my dad.*

Whatever happens, that won't ever change.

Friends

It was weird going to school on Monday.

Everyone came rushing over to me in homeroom, asking for details: Did I run away from home? Where did I go? Was I with Kai? Why did I sneak off without telling anyone? Did I get in trouble?

The strange thing was how all of it—the play, my makeup, the *RESERVED* sign, and even Comic Con and Cat FX—felt like it had happened months ago, to someone else. Even when I explained it all to Poppy, it was like I was describing a video I'd watched. Although I didn't tell her about Mom—not yet. Not at school, in front of everyone.

Seeing Kai in math made some of it seem real. He walked over to my desk and gave me a small, uncertain smile. "You okay, Wren?"

I shrugged.

"Yeah, me too," he said.

"You got in trouble?"

"Yeah. Dad took away my phone for three months. Also my computer."

"For three months? Wow, that's harsh."

"Nah, I deserved it." He lowered his voice to a murmur. "And your mom?"

"We think she'll be okay, but after the hospital she's going into rehab. For pain pills."

I took a few seconds. Actually saying those words to a friend made me feel almost dizzy. But mostly it was a big relief.

"My dad flew out yesterday," I added. "He's staying with me."

Kai nodded. "That's good, right?"

"A little weird, but yeah. It is."

"Well, if you ever want to talk . . ." His eyes met mine. His two different-colored eyes, which weren't ghost eyes at all. Not really.

"Thank you, Kai," I told him. "You're a very good friend."

The way he smiled at me then, I could tell I didn't need to worry about the crush anymore.

o O o

On the way home from school, I told Poppy about Mom too. It was a relief that she didn't ask too many questions, because it wasn't like I had answers.

But she did ask one question—*Are you still mad at your mom?*—that made me catch my breath. Because of course Mom wasn't some kind of preprogrammed robot—she could make her choices about her body, couldn't she? Plus she was a nurse, *a health professional*, so she should have known she had a problem and gotten help for it, right?

And then there was all the lying that she did. Over and over. To *me*.

"Yeah, I guess I'm still mad," I admitted. "But to be honest, mostly I'm scared."

"I know," Poppy said.

For a second I waited for the *but*: *But don't worry. But everything will be fine.* Because Poppy was from a very different family.

Except she was too good a friend to act fake cheery, or to pretend she could see into the future, or had information I didn't.

So instead of talking, what she did was throw her arm around my shoulders and walk me all the way to my door.

Forward Motion

A few days later, Mom left Donwood General Hospital detox and entered an inpatient treatment place—the Glendale Center for Rehabilitation—about forty miles away.

That same afternoon, Dad brought me to see a therapist, a cool woman named Dionna whose scruffy dog, Hank, cuddled with me on her sofa. Mostly we talked about Cyrus and Lola, and also about special-effects makeup—but at the end of the hour, she asked about Mom, and I told her about Glendale. Not that I knew a whole lot, but it still felt good to tell a dog-loving person like Dionna.

One night almost a week later, Dad came into my bedroom while I was sort-of-doing homework.

"Wren," he said softly. "Are you busy? Is this an okay time to talk?"

"Sure." I shut my math notebook.

He sat on the edge of my bed. "Mom's feeling better now, and we're making arrangements for you to visit her at Glendale. But I wanted to give you a heads-up, so you're prepared. Sometimes after the twenty-one-day program, patients transfer somewhere else."

I stared at him. "Like where? You mean to another twenty-one-day program?"

"Well, the other programs her doctors are recommending are sixty days and ninety days."

Which means two months and three months.

My throat stung. "Why so long? Can't the doctors at Glendale just cure her *now*?"

"Sweetheart, recovery from opioid addiction can be a long, hard road, so we all just want to give Mom the best chance to get well and stay that way. Nothing's been decided yet, okay? There are lots of details we have to work out." Dad clasped and unclasped his hands. "But if she does do an extended stay after this one, I'll need to get back to Vanessa and the babies. And we'll have to think about you relocating to Brooklyn."

"Relocating?" The word bounced around my brain. "You mean I'll have to go live with you?"

"Yes, until Mom's ready to come home. We won't know the plan for a while."

Oh. Oh no.

Well, but if it's what Mom needs. To get well and stay that way.

I wiped my eyes with my hand. It was hard to talk. "What about Dionna?"

"Possibly she does telemedicine. If not, there are tons of good therapists in Brooklyn. Actually, Brooklyn is like therapist headquarters. You can't cross the street without bumping into one."

He smiled a little. I didn't.

"What about Lulu and Cyrus?" I asked.

"Krystal says she'll take care of them," Dad said quietly. "But let's not get ahead of ourselves, okay? Like I said, nothing's been decided yet. Let's see where we are in a couple of weeks."

I just nodded, because here was another choice I didn't have.

As soon as Dad left my room, I texted Poppy and Kai with the news.

A minute later Poppy answered: Wren, we may vacation in NYC this summer!!! If you're there I could visit you in Bklyn!!! 😊😊

And Kai answered: Huh. Well, I hope you won't have to go. But I'm already planning cosplay for the next Comic Con. So we shd talk about that, okay?

Four days later, Krystal and Dad brought me to visit Mom at Glendale. At first, when Dad told me we were going, I panicked. Because what if Mom and Dad had another one of their big shouty fights? If I was stuck in a room with them, I wouldn't be able to tune them out, research makeup colors or whatever.

But Dad explained they were both coming just to be there for me; he wouldn't go inside to see Mom, he said, and neither would Krystal.

I asked if he didn't want to visit Mom.

Of course he did, and he would, he answered. Not this time. Not yet. But soon.

"You ready for this, honey?" Krystal asked as Dad and I got into her car, him in the passenger seat, me in the rear with my bulging backpack.

"I'm not sure," I admitted. "I actually don't know what to say to her."

"Well, I know your mom will be happy just to see you! And of course it's natural to feel a bit nervous."

Dad turned around. His eyes met mine. "We all have a bunch of complicated feelings right now, jellybean. But for today, try to be positive, and see what happens."

"What happens?" I repeated stupidly.

"Yeah. Just follow Mom's lead."

I stared out the window. Forward motion, a blur of trees and buildings and shopping malls.

Who knows what I'll see at the end? I thought, wishing

that someone would tell me a bunch of steps to follow, one after the other, like a makeup video. *First you do this part, and then you do that. . . . In twenty-one days, this will happen, and then this.*

Maybe a lot more of this.

But Cat FX said you had to improvise sometimes. And even when you didn't, even when all you had to do was follow directions, sometimes a step was missing. A secret ingredient. And you had to do the best you could with what you had.

Krystal turned on the radio for the weather. Seventy-three degrees at eleven o'clock, hotter than it should be in April. *Glad I wore shorts,* I thought, even though the car's AC gave my bare legs goose bumps.

About an hour later we pulled up to a boring office building in a "corporate campus," which was really just a bunch of boring office buildings in a big parking lot.

This was it?

"It's sort of cozy inside," Krystal said, reading my mind. "Don't worry, Wren; it'll be fine."

"But where will you guys be?" My voice cracked a little.

"Your dad will get you checked in, and then we'll both hang out in the lobby."

I went cold. "Dad, you *sure* you don't want to come in with me?"

His eyes were gentle as he did a hand sandwich. "No, jellybean. Today is just for the two of you. Mom-and-daughter time."

I took a breath, grabbed my backpack, and stepped out of the car.

Mermaid

Inside the Glendale Center for Rehabilitation a pretty nurse named Fiona wearing pink scrubs met me in the waiting area. Then she led me into a small room with a couple of fake leather chairs and four pastel-colored paintings of flowers on the walls. Between the chairs was a small round table with a box of tissues.

Fiona smiled. "Would you like some cocoa? Or water?"

Too hot for cocoa. I bit my dry lips. "Water would be good, thanks."

Fiona brought me some lukewarm water in a small, waxy Dixie cup. I drank it in one gulp as I sat in the sticky chair with my backpack wedged between my sweaty knees.

Then she looked up from some charts she was filling out and smiled at me again. "Okay, Wren. Can you tell me when you're turning thirteen?"

Huh? "July twenty-ninth," I said.

"Well, our rule is that for kids under thirteen a nurse must be present during family visits. I'm sorry," she added, actually looking sorry.

A couple of minutes went by. The clock on the wall made a sound like *blip-blip-blip*, almost in time to my thumping heart.

And then, all at once, Mom was there. Inside the room with Fiona and me. Wearing her faded taco-restaurant tee and yoga pants.

"Honeybee," she cried.

I sprang from the chair to hug her. We stayed like that for a while, me inhaling her soapy smell. Plus something else.

"You smell good," I said, feeling a little shy for some reason.

"Mmm, thanks. Aromatherapy," Mom explained. "We're big fans of dried lavender around here."

We sat. Mom's dark eyes sparkled—maybe from tears? But she was grinning.

"So, dahling, we rendezvous at last," she said in her Hollywood diva voice.

"Yes, dahling. Nice chairs," I said. "The pleather feels absolutely divine against my legs."

"Only the finest pleather, dahling." She pointed. "Hey,

what's in that backpack? Did you bring me Phish Food?"

"Next time. Today I brought you something better." I unzipped the front pocket. "Supplies," I said, dumping a bunch of products on the table. Foundations and pigments, liners and shadows, lipsticks and blushes. Not just from the Mom shoebox. From Vanessa's makeup case too.

"Ooh, goody," Mom said, clapping her hands like a little kid. "Hey, I have a brilliant idea—can you make me Bride of Frankenstein, so I can scare all the doctors?"

I laughed. Then I glanced at Fiona, who was either concentrating hard on her charts or just pretending. "Well, we *could* do Bride of Frankenstein. But I dunno. I'm feeling more mermaid today. And now I know why it never looked right."

"Oh yeah? Why is that?"

"Because Cat FX left something out. On purpose."

"She did? How very sneaky of her, dahling. Well, we'll do our own private mermaid, then. Although maybe just a simple one, because we don't have a lot of time."

I got to work. Foundation, Blue Violet. The right colors, but not all the details.

Mom always kept her face still better than anyone else. But after a few minutes, I guess she was thinking about the *blip-blip-blip* of the clock, and how this "family visit" wasn't allowed to last more than an hour. So she asked how Dad and Vanessa were.

"You want me to talk behind their back?" I asked.

Mom's eyebrows knitted. "Oh, Wren—"

"I'm just teasing," I said quickly. "They're both good. So are the babies. And you know, Dad and Vanessa really care about you."

"Yes, I know that," Mom said softly. Suddenly her face pinched. "Listen, honeybee. There's something I have to tell you. I wish I didn't, but it's part of what I have to do."

"Okay," I said.

I could see Mom's chest rise and fall as she breathed. "All right," she said. "So here it is. There was never any Emily. I made up a housecleaner so there'd be someone to blame. But I was the one who took your money. Because I needed cash. For pills."

I didn't say anything. The truth was, by now I'd figured Mom took the money, but it was such a horrible thought that I'd just stuffed it under my bed.

Mom closed her eyes for a long second. Then she looked into my face. "Wren, I didn't *intend* to take it; I was searching your room for makeup, because I was upset about Vanessa sending you stuff in secret. And when I found that pretty makeup kit under your bed, I opened it. And saw all those bills."

"Okay," I said again, like it was the only word in my vocabulary.

"I just wasn't thinking straight at the time, sweetheart. And I know it's not good enough, I know it doesn't change what happened, what I did, or how I lied to you. But please believe that I'm so, so sorry. Do you think you can forgive me?"

I nodded. There would be a time to tell her how I felt— and not just about the money. About all of it.

Not this time. Not yet. But soon.

"All right, good." Mom smiled—a nervous flicker of a smile. She glanced at Fiona, who was still writing in her charts. "So anyway, sweetheart, what's going on with you? I feel like I've skipped a few chapters."

As I brushed some Blue Violet on her cheeks, I told her about the show and about Kai, leaving out the part about Comic Con for now.

"He's a good friend," I said.

"This was the boy whose heart you broke?"

She remembered our conversation on Valentine's Day. I'd been wondering about this—how much she remembered. How much was just lost.

"Yeah, same kid," I said.

"So, in other words, he healed."

"I guess."

Mom did a hand sandwich. "People heal, sweetheart. We feel things, and then feelings change. People change.

All the time." She kissed my cheek with blue lips. "Just promise you'll be the true Wren, whoever that is. Feeling all your feelings, whatever they are. Or aren't."

"I promise."

"Even if that means you're still mad at *me*." Now her eyes were big and soft, full of question marks. She was asking what was in my heart, and this time I knew I couldn't just nod. I had to answer.

But with what words?

"Mom, I love you," I said. "And yes, I was mad at you about some things. But not anymore."

Was that true? Had I really stopped being mad at Mom? Maybe I'd feel different as soon as I was back in the car, heading to Donwood, and possibly to Brooklyn, and to whatever came after that. Everything could change, nothing was decided, and there was no step-by-step how-to video for all the days ahead.

But one thing was sure. Right at that moment, in that small room, sitting in those fake-leather seats, I was feeling nothing more complicated than love.

"And now stop talking while I fix your lipstick," I said.

Acknowledgments

Heartfelt thanks once again to my superb editor, Alyson Heller, and to the all-star team at Aladdin—Valerie Garfield, Kristin Gilson, Michelle Leo, Chelsea Morgan, Sarah Woodruff, Amy Beaudoin, Nicole Benevento, and Amanda Livingston. Thanks to Karen Sherman for a masterful round of copyediting (though any remaining errors are my own).

Erika Pajarillo, thank you for another extraordinary cover. Heather Palisi, thank you for another beautiful design.

I couldn't do this without the wisdom and guidance of my agent, Jill Grinberg, and her brilliant team at Jill Grinberg Literary Management, especially Sam Farkas, Sophia Seidner, and Denise Page.

Tracey Daniels, Casey Blackwell, and Karen Wadsworth of Media Masters Publicity, I'm so grateful for your energy and passion.

Thanks to Amanda Sklar for demonstrating special-effects makeup, and for recommending YouTube videos.

Thanks to addiction specialist Nicholas Lessa, MA, LCSW, CASAC, of INTER-CARE Westchester, for

generously sharing expertise about opioid addiction. Thanks to Kristina Manich, MSN, RN-BC, for talking to me about the New York-Presbyterian Westchester Behavioral Health Center in White Plains's inpatient substance abuse program.

Special thanks to my family—Chris, Josh, Alex and Dani, Lizzy and Jamie—for endless support and encouragement. Bonus thanks to Chris and Lizzy for tactful, incisive editorial feedback. I love you all.

Here's a sneak peek at
BARBARA DEE's
next novel!

Author of *Maybe He Just Likes You*

BARBARA DEE

HAVEN JACOBS
SAVES THE
PLANET

SENSITIVE

Sometimes in the middle of the night when I couldn't sleep, I'd think about the time I lost my family in a bouncy castle.

It happened at a state fair—a million years ago, when I was like four or five. We'd all been bouncing, having a great time, when suddenly my big brother, Carter, said his stomach felt funny. I watched my family race out of the castle, shouting for me to follow. But I wasn't ready to go, so I just kept on bouncing, all by myself.

Finally I stepped out of the castle to the flat, unbouncy ground, expecting to see Mom, Dad, and Carter.

Except they weren't there.

No family.

For a second I froze, panicking. And then I started running.

I ran over to the Ferris wheel, then the roller coaster, then the ice cream stand where we'd all bought extra-large swirly cones an hour before. I ran over to a water-gun game where the prize was a giant stuffed Pikachu, then to the stage where some guy was playing a banjo, and past a lady in a cowgirl dress who was selling pies.

Somehow I made it back to the bouncy castle—and when I got there, my family was waiting. They looked terrified.

"Haven, what happened to you?" Dad yelled, and Mom burst into tears as she squeezed me tight.

"If you ever get separated from us, just stay put," she scolded when she finally stopped crying. "Promise you won't move around next time; let *us* find *you*."

I promised. But I remember thinking how silly that was. I mean, *of course* I'd try to find them! Because staying put just seemed so helpless and babyish. I needed to *do* something, not stand there waiting, like a stuffed Pikachu on a shelf.

"Haven's a true problem solver," Grandpa Aaron used to say.

"Yes, but not everything is a true problem," Mom would answer.

She'd talk to me about "learning to relax," "having patience," "accepting what we can't control." And Dad would talk about "enjoying the process." About "good sportsmanship," too, when I'd lose at *Blaster Force 3* to Carter or miss an easy goal in soccer.

"Haven, games are not about the final score," he'd tell me. "It's important to just have fun."

And I'd think: *Okay, but what's fun about losing?* To me, things counted only when I knew how they added up, or how they ended. So getting to the end of something—the solution of a puzzle, the last chapter in a book, the final scene in a movie—was basically why I was doing it in the first place.

I didn't try explaining this to Mom and Dad because I knew what they'd say: *Haven, honey, you should try to relax—enjoy the process!*

Although, to be fair, they didn't *only* talk this way, and sometimes they took my side. Like they did last summer, right before seventh grade, when our family went camping at Lake Exeter. I'd never gone fishing before, so I was excited to go out on the water with Dad and Carter. I even caught a trout in the first half hour.

Except the thing was, until the very second I caught

that trout, somehow I hadn't realized that catching a fish meant killing it.

"Can't we just throw it back?" I'd begged Dad.

"Come on, Haven, fish are food," Dad had replied.

"Not to me! I'm not a fish killer!"

Because how could I have eaten this creature that was still twitching and staring at me, that just a minute earlier I'd felt tugging on my rod? I absolutely couldn't. And I didn't want anyone else to eat it either.

"Aw, honey," Dad said to me. "Don't worry, fish don't have feelings."

"How do you know that?" By then I was almost crying.

Carter groaned. "Argh, Haven, why can't you just enjoy the lake! And being on this boat. You're missing the point of this whole vacation!"

"No, I'm not! Because the *point* of being on this boat is killing animals!"

"That's not the point at all! Why do you always have to make such a big deal about everything? And get so *emotional*?"

"All right, enough squabbling, you two," Dad said. "You'll scare off the other trout."

"Good, I hope we do," I said.

Right at that moment, without saying anything, Dad

threw the fish back. If he was annoyed with me, he didn't show it, but Carter did.

That night, as we ate a takeout supper back at our campsite, my brother announced, "I can't believe we came all the way here *to fish*, but because of Haven, we're eating ramen."

"Carter, you don't even like eating fish," Mom said. "And you love ramen! We all do," she added as she caught my eye.

Carter slurped some noodles. "Not the point. Haven's so hypersensitive. She can't relax about *anything*!"

"All right, Carter, you've shared your opinion; now let it go," Dad said sharply.

Mom changed the subject, but I didn't pay attention. Instead I was thinking how the lake was big, full of fish. Plenty of other people were still fishing. I'd saved the trout, but how much had I accomplished, really?

Plus I'd messed up my family's vacation, and now my brother was mad at me.

So even though I tried hard to enjoy myself—and the last few days of vacation before seventh grade—it felt like I'd won and lost at the same time.

ANTARCTICA

Of course I didn't say this to my brother, but even before that fishing trip I'd been thinking about bigger things than what we were eating for supper. I'd been thinking about the planet—all the scary stuff happening with climate change.

And not just thinking about it: worrying. Reading stories on my computer. Having bad dreams sometimes, like the one where a tornado tore the roof off our house. Another one about my favorite elm tree catching fire, and how I couldn't save a nest of baby robins. Another one about my bed floating away after a big rainstorm.

But I didn't talk about it, because I didn't want to hear how I was being "too sensitive," "too emotional," focusing on a problem-that-wasn't-really-a-problem.

Until one day in the spring of seventh grade, when our teacher Mr. Hendricks showed a video in science class. It was about Antarctica, how climate change was making the glaciers disappear.

At first I didn't get what the narrator was talking about, because he had an English accent and called them *glassy-ers*. But when I realized he meant *glay-shers*, and that they were melting in front of our eyes—right underneath the penguins—I got a funny buzzing feeling in my head.

If the glaciers melt, what happens to those penguins? I thought.

Don't ask me where this question came from. I mean, it wasn't like I was this penguin-obsessed person. I'd always *liked* penguins—the way they waddled and swam, the way both penguin parents took turns holding the eggs on their feet. But to be honest, I'd never really *thought* about them before.

And now this English guy in the video was talking about giant chunks of ice crashing into the ocean, meaning the Antarctic was in trouble. And that meant the penguins were in trouble, and probably the whales and the seals, too.

Also dolphins, right? Plus a million creatures and plants whose names I didn't even know.

Just then I remembered the trout, how we almost killed it for no good reason. And that made me think how humans were killing everything for no reason. How the whole planet—animals, plants, lakes, oceans, towns, cities—was in danger.

Including people. Including my family. And my friends.

Maybe our town would be swept up in a giant hurricane, and our school would sink. And our house would wash away while I was sleeping in my bed. Not just like in a scary dream, but *in real life*.

Suddenly I couldn't breathe. My chest got tight and I was sweating all over: my armpits, my hands, my scalp. One word flashed in my brain—*Run!*—and before I knew what I was doing, I ran out of the classroom to hide in the girls' restroom for the last four minutes of the period.

But even as I stood in front of the mirror, splashing cold water on my face, my brain kept replaying the video of that glacier crashing into the ocean, the penguins and other animals in danger. Like it was at the top of my mental playlist and I couldn't scroll past it. Or delete it. Or reboot.

At lunch my best friend, Riley, asked if I was all right. But it was hard to think of an answer that sounded normal.

"It's nothing," I said.

Riley's eyes were round and serious. "Come on, Haven. *Something's* going on; I can see it on your face. Just tell me, okay?"

I dipped a carrot stick in my hummus, making small circles. "Okay, so. It's that video we watched in science. It kind of freaked me out, actually."

"And that's why you left the room?"

I nodded.

"Yeah, I thought that was maybe it." Riley pulled the crust off her sandwich, making a crust pile on her napkin. "But how come it upset you so much? Because Mr. Hendricks is always showing us stuff like that, right?"

"Yeah," I admitted. "But this was different."

"Why?"

"I don't know, I just can't stop thinking about the penguins! Didn't it seem like they could almost *tell* the ice was melting under their feet? And that they couldn't do anything to stop it?"

"I guess," Riley said. "They do seem really smart, don't they? The way they communicate—"

"But it wasn't *just* the penguins. It was everything *else* in that video too. What's happening to the whales and dolphins. What's happening to Antarctica. An entire *continent*."

Riley blinked at me. I knew that lately she was scared

about her grandma's heart problems. If she was scared about climate stuff too, she'd never told me. And the truth was, we only talked about other stuff. School stuff, people stuff. Not this.

But now I couldn't shut up. "And it's not like we can go, 'Oh, it's Antarctica, a zillion miles away; it doesn't matter to us.' Because *of course* it does—climate change affects the whole planet! And we're all just sitting here, eating lunch, like *ho hum, just another boring school day.*"

Riley pushed away her sandwich and nibbled a chocolate chip off her cookie. "Okay, I'm not arguing with you, Haven. What are we supposed to do about it, though?"

"I'm not sure! But don't you think there has to be *something*? Because I hate just feeling so . . . helpless."

My voice was too loud, I could tell. A few tables over, Archer looked up at me. The two of us were still friends, I reminded myself, even if lately he'd been avoiding me at school.

"Okay if I sit here?" Without waiting for an answer, Ember Faraday was at our table, squeezing in next to Riley. "What are you talking about? You both look so *serious.*"

The way she said it was definitely a criticism.

I tried to catch Riley's eye. We used to have the same opinion of Ember, who everyone called Em. Before middle school she'd always acted like we had permanent head lice.

Then the big factory in town closed, her best friends' families moved away—and now, for some reason I didn't get, she'd started hanging out with Riley. Which meant hanging out with me.

I chewed what was left of my thumbnail.

"Oh, we're just talking about this video we saw in science," Riley told Em. Her whole face lit up, the way it always did when Ember Faraday was around. "Haven's pretty upset about it, so."

"Really?" Em smiled at me like I was a toddler. "How come, Haven?"

I switched to my pointer nail. "I don't know. Stuff about animals in danger always freaks me out, I guess."

"It was about Antarctica," Riley told her. "The melting glaciers, and what'll happen to all the penguins."

"Got it." Em pulled the top off her blueberry yogurt and licked the foil. "Okay, so tell me about this penguin video."

"It wasn't a *penguin video*," I said.

Em raised her eyebrows. "But penguins were *in* it?"

"A little. Mostly they were hiding from the camera." I looked at Riley to back me up, but she was playing with her crust pile.

"Wait, I don't understand," Em said. "Riley, didn't you say Haven was upset about—"

"The video was about climate change," I said through

my teeth. "*Not* just penguins. What it means for the *entire planet*. Including us."

"Oh. Well, *that's* depressing."

"Haven wants to do something to help," Riley explained.

Em licked a blob of purple yogurt off her spoon. "Like what, Haven? Another one of your projects?"

She meant the petition I'd started back in the fall to get more veggie food on the lunchroom menu. And the car wash I'd organized to raise money for the local SPCA. And possibly the bake sale I did with Riley in sixth grade to support an elephant sanctuary in Florida. We'd raised fifty-eight dollars, although half of that was from our parents.

"That's not what I mean," I said. "I just want to do something that *actually matters*."

Now Em was giving me her *aren't you adorable* smile again.

"Well, I'm sure if anyone can save the planet, it's definitely *you*, Haven," she said.

About the Author

BARBARA DEE is the author of thirteen middle-grade novels published by Simon & Schuster, including *My Life in the Fish Tank, Maybe He Just Likes You, Everything I Know About You, Halfway Normal,* and *Star-Crossed*. Her books have earned several starred reviews and have been named to many best-of lists, including the Washington Post Best Children's Books, the ALA Notable Children's Books, the ALA Rise: A Feminist Book Project List, the NCSS-CBC Notable Social Studies Trade Books for Young People, and the ALA Rainbow Book List Top Ten. Barbara lives with her family, including a naughty cat named Luna and a sweet rescue hound dog named Ripley, in Westchester County, New York.

CHECK OUT THESE AMAZING BOOKS FROM
BARBARA DEE!

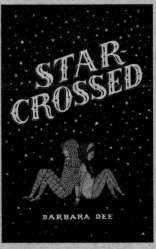

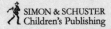

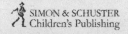